BC¹

A CODA:

THE GO LOVE QUARTET

BC¹

A CODA:

THE GO LOVE QUARTET

Michael Gills

Lake Dallas, Texas

Requests for permission to reprint or reuse material
from this work should be sent to:

Permissions
Madville Publishing
PO Box 358
Lake Dallas, TX 75065

Cover Design: Kim Davis
Cover Photo: Lyra Gills
Author Photo: Kim Davis
With thanks to Jill Gills for proofreading

ISBN: 978-1-963695-51-9 paperback
978-1-963695-52-6 ebook

Library of Congress Control Number: 2025947027

*As ever, for Jill and Lyra
with all my love*

BC[1]

A Coda:

The Go Love Quartet

SYNOPSIS

This is the fifth novel of the *Go Love Quartet*, a Coda to end the sequence.

The first book, *Emergency Instructions*, tells how Renee Harvell is bewildered by the South. People are named Peck Titsworth, for Christ's sake, and every curve in the road hides a dead dog or a "Prepare to meet God" or a "Trust the One Who Bled for You" sign. The novel opens with the young Harvell family's arrival in Arkansas during the "summer of death," and follows their struggle to survive in a place where "practitioners of backwoods witchcraft are as common as Methodists and sometimes one in the same."

Joey's been hired as Assistant Professor of History with a specialty in southern conflicts involving Mormons, and Renee teaches Special-Ed at R'Ville Middle. When her life intertwines with Rhonda Love, whose daughter was savagely murdered the summer before, a moment of reckoning flies toward them and their men. Like the far-off thrum that ever thumps from the backside of their property, the Harvell's year in the Natural State takes on a heartbeat all its own. What happens is as unpredictable as the mystery lights that hover above the Ozarks that winter, when country women hang snakes from tree limbs to tease out rain that finally comes gushing. *Emergency Instructions* plumbs blood ties and roots, the inescapable connectedness to place and kin.

Go Love, the second and title book of the quartet, finds the Harvell family in Melbourne Beach, Florida, for a birthday party that morphs into a funeral when Joey's adoptive father calls after midnight with the news: "Mama drowned of a heart attack." Josephine Harvell had never been lucky in love; from Buddy Washer, the Arizona mistake, who got her pregnant and was arrested trying to smuggle weed in the belly of a Santa Clause suit, to O.W., a truck driving brawler who pawns everything including her sewing machine to cover bets, she knows and knows that love isn't easy.

The young family has to steal their rental car and drive to Arkansas where *Go Love's* muddy relationships finally twist together amidst the tensions of a southern funeral. This all happens in Lonoke County, Arkansas, once pummeled by the great tornado of 1976, when the bank and post office got hit and townsfolk's stamped letters flew up into the airstream, finding their ways to the glittering icefields of Canada. On the Dixie Circuit, where it was nothing for a semi to pull into town to exhibit a two-hundred-pound rat, or donkey woman nursing horsey-faced twins. Anything at all's possible in such a place. Just as the black women shout out during the funeral, *Go Love* is the command the novel's inhabitants must finally live by, even when life offers up a truckload of reasons to do the contrary. Even it if kills us—go love.

West, book three of the *Go Love Quartet*, closes the circle initiated when Josephine Stepwell made the star-crossed decision to head west with the outlaw husband who'd lied up one side of her heart and down the other. Now, her granddaughter, who grew up sneaking peeks at a dwarf uncle's photo in her father's black Bible, runs away from her Utah home to Arizona, where she meets Davey the Dwarf in a south side Tucson bar catering to washed up professional wrestlers.

There, with fellow dropout non-Mormon Jack, she is reunited with her long-lost kith and kin, standing in for Joey who'd promised the blood father he'd never met that he'd return. Only he never did. In the meantime, grandfather Buddy'd died, was buried in a cemetery with all the rest of the Washers, and it's there the circle finally closes, with champagne and hard words at the graveside. Steeped in the Stepwell disasters of love, *West* interweaves the strands left hanging in the Quartet's first two novels. It offers peace to those who have departed in a world of hurt.

Dialing the three previous novels' tendency toward theatrical catastrophe up to 11, *New Harmony*, the fourth novel of the *Go Love Quartet*, traces the Stepwell history of hurt and tragedy and loss, arriving at, if only temporarily, a fragile harmony that allows the present to be reconciled with the past.

Pursued west, Edgar Paris can't outrun his past. He ends up in an Arizona jail for "defamation of distinguished persons as manifest at heritage sites," not to mention slander and assault on an officer of the peace. Joey Harvell must bring Edgar home but before they return the two will have to confront the bloody legacy of Navajo Bridge, *aka* John Doyle Lee Bridge, originally named for the lone man convicted for the Mountain Meadows Massacre, the single worst mass murder of whites from Manifest Destiny.

Amplifying the three previous books' generational violence, the Harvell family tries for all they're worth to make a home with roots in foreign ground, just as the ill-fated Fancher party had, and Mormons who'd retreated from Missouri, and endless emigrants who ever walked west toward the promise of a new life. *New Harmony* culminates the Quartet by trumpeting its namesake: *Go Love*, the one buoy that will ever rescue us.

Bringing the novel sequence to a fiery close, BC^1 lays down the Harvell grudge of Mountain Meadows and aims, finally, at healing for all involved. Lara Luce Harvell has been charged with carrying her late father's prized Martin D-28, handmade in Nazareth, Pennsylvania in 1998, the same year she was born, to Mr. Edgar Paris in Dinnehotso, Arizona. Such is repayment to him for saving Joey's right index finger when it got bit off in an Arkansas fight. The resulting journey, part dynamite, revenge, and the tenderness of love, wanders into the lands of the woolly-headed Washers, a whole tribe of wandering relatives who "inhabited the desert, living in trailer parks from Tuba City to Las Vegas, pumping five dollars' worth of regular at a time into jalopies that overheated and ran on threadbare tires." Not unlike the rural south where this sequence all started, Rez land on the border of Utah and Arizona is dog eat dog. Life offers few legal ways to get by. Whites and Indians eye each other with mistrust, and young people either move to Las Vegas or Tucson or sunny California, or get reduced to doing whatever it takes. Yazz Begay and Louie Washer are no exceptions. When they stumble on a stash of newly-buried dynamite while spray-painting graffiti in a burial cave, what else is there to do but find a buyer, ring the big bell and move to Hawaii, drink Mai Tais on Waikiki? But the man's ever out there, sniffing them out, just like he had their mothers and fathers. High school dropouts with the taste of siphoned gas in their mouths, what else was there to do but meanness? Roll on down the highway to hell. *Koyanisqatsi*, the Diné called it, *world out of balance*.

Luce has no idea what she's stepping into when she knocks on Big Rose Begay's front door on Mother's Day weekend, her own mom on the other side of the continent, ever staring off the beach access stairway to the sea—mourning. Whatever Mountain Meadows had meant to her father, it had ended with his ashes back at the family cemetery in Solgahatchia on the Trail of Tears. She'd brought the Martin, made good on the promise. What Edgar and Rose, who was expecting, did with it was their own business.

In *BC1*, the dazed travelers—like so many before them—make one last run for California and its hope for renewal. They escape for the time being whatever it is that has dogged them all the way. Then, as in all great quests, Luce must turn back toward home, with little but prayer and the newly won knowledge of what matters most in this world as guide.

BC¹

PROLOGUE

After all the mess with Navajo Bridge, it'd been Edgar's job to get rid of the dynamite. A hundred and forty sticks in holes drilled into the Moenkopi, each one with the name of a dearly departed written on it in fine point Sharpie. Of course, they couldn't just leave it there. What were they thinking? Always the potential for violence, Harvell offered. Malarkey. It could go off. Somebody'd get hurt. Stoner'd get wind of it, change his mind and come sniffing around. The holes were in the abutment on either end of the bridge. It's not like he had to suspend from the middle or rappel or get fancy with ropes or anything. And Rita gave him cover from up there on the pedestrian bridge, selling her mojos with big Kuya on her lap, flash a mirror if the man comes, tell him when to knock it off with hammer and chisel. Warn him if the devil-birds flap-flapped up under the spangles. Three days it took him, packed them in liquor store boxes stuffed with Daily Suns. Wrapped with packing tape and all sealed in hefties. Rose had helped him load by moonlight, and they'd driven it over Black Mesa to Dinnehotso on New Year's Eve, drums over tribal radio going boom, boom, boom. Rose Begay, a schoolteacher over to Monument Valley, medicine people had buried her birth placenta in the schoolyard, and a holy man prophesied she'd one day return to teach a new generation, so the language of the Diné would not perish but have everlasting life.

1

It'd been Rose Edgar'd hallucinated when Stoner whomped him upside the head. She'd been dressed in her Native American University of Utah regalia, wearing a wealth of turquoise and porcupine quill, borne up on the wings of that mutant angel bird, fierce white cross zigzagged on its underside.

"What do we do with it now?" she asked when they hit Monument Valley.

A little further was Big Rose's house, and the matrilineal way of families that Edgar would have no more guessed than the man in the moon, where a woman takes a man into her clan because they've been kicked out of their own, how it was with the Navajo on the Diné Nation which straddled Utah and New Mexico and Arizona, ancestral home of the Hopi and Chiricahua to the south, medicine land bounded by the Lukachukai and Chuska on one side, Sleeping Ute on the other, Bear's Ears to the north and the Grand Fucking Canyon to the West.

Like her mother, Rose Begay smelled of fry bread. And pinyon and nighttime when the frost comes and the breath steams in front of your face. A fire was burning down in the hollow past Laguna Creek. Edgar smelled it through the barely cracked hut window.

"Tomorrow's New Year's," he said. "Can we decide then?"

She'd laugh at anything, Rose Begay.

"What's so funny?"

She opened the door, got out and pointed. Edgar's headlights splashed clean to the bridge and beyond, where smoke was rising, the place that would be his home for a while now, though he didn't know that yet.

She said, "Race."

And just like that out under the gauzy wedge of sky, the Indian princess was running, laughing as she went, hauling ass, and Edgar ever after her, the dogs not yet onto them.

That's how this starts—the story of Edgar and Rose, how

her daddy used to get off work on a Friday afternoon and drive them from Aneth over to Big Rose's in Dinnehotso, only they'd drive up to the river bridge on the Utah side outside Mexican Water and Daddy'd pull over a good hundred yards from the Arizona state line, see who could cross first.

"Race," he'd say, and there they'd go, splashed in headlights.

Edgar'd learn to make the story his own. In time, he would. But there was the matter of the dynamite in Yukon Jack and Crown and Old Crow boxes stacked in the bed of the truck. If they only could have kept running, down through creek bed toward the fire and lives burning before them, fry bread baking in a stone oven heated by pinyon.

She'd beat him across, laughing big frosty breaths, the silver of her voice clean as skim ice on Laguna Creek at first light on a good day.

PART ONE

1.

She'd told him, her aunt by blood, that there were others like Daddy, children born of mothers lured to Arizona under false pretense. She'd called them by name. Boys and girls whose mother's escapes had been blocked, long grown into men and women. And by now they'd have children of their own, and those children children, so that a whole tribe of wandering Washers inhabited the desert, living in trailer parks from Tuba City to Las Vegas, pumping five dollars' worth of regular at a time into jalopies that overheated and ran on threadbare tires, whose tags were expired and inspection stickers had been razorbladed off license plates in bowling alley parking lots where some got caught, hit in the head with tire tools and never had the wounds stitched, so there'd be a pink welt just under the hairline that would catch on Sunday mornings before cracked bathroom mirrors. Whose crooked teeth had never been straightened. Cavities neither filled nor rootcanaled. Parents to whom dentists would say, "You're dooming your child to dentures," before the extraction, so the mamas would weep and wish themselves dead. A vast woolly-headed people who wouldn't know each other from Adam.

That's what she was thinking, Lucy Harvell, driving the gravel road toward Lanty, the rusted gate of the family cemetery in the rearview mirror, behind her now for good and ever with Daddy's ashes. The crying had done her good. She could think now that the thing was done. Light rain, a whiff of tire rubber on the breeze, just like he said there would be. On barbed-wire fences, white blackberry blooms, and the brown-eyed Susans from here to tomorrow. All that collective weight behind her now. Save the D-28. He'd bought it the summer of 1998, the year she was born, so the Martin would be the same age as Luce from here on out. Hand made in Nazareth, Pennsylvania, it lay back there on the green velvet inside the black case. A thief's dream for pawning, he'd left few instructions: *keep humidified, don't give to boyfriend, loosen strings if you fly.*

Learn to play.

Behind her now in the backseat of the Subaru, covered with a beach towel Mom had given her for the very purpose, his fingerprints still on the silver tuning pegs, mewing a little on the gravel road back to the highway.

If you need to turn loose of, take to Mr. Edgar T. Paris, Dinnehotso, AZ.

At Solgahatchia, she turns south onto blacktop, where a bullet ridden sign of an Indian on horseback says WELCOME TO THE AUTHENTIC TRAIL OF TEARS. Raining still, the afternoon sun burns through the clouds, making the whole green world seem awash with her father's odd magic, even the sad-eyed Indian on his shot-up horse. She'd been there before, Arizona, had people in Tucson, if the old dwarf still lived. On Daddy's beat atlas, Arizona on one side, Arkansas on the other, so the two touched when the book closed.

Words written on one page have bled onto the other.

Technically, she lived here in Arkansas when she was a toddler. They'd owned a four-bedroom ranch when Daddy'd moved them back home from Utah to be *professor in the cow pasture,* his words. She could remember blips and flashes, Lara Luce, the stories and history of their time there she'd heard at the dinner table late into happy hours, when the repetitions turned it all into the sort of myth dad could hang his hat on, put his unrootedness at ease. The time they'd taken her to Long Pool with

Meemaw and Poppy, up from Florida, and she'd splish-splashed just off the bank and swallowed the feces-laden water, which of course they didn't know about and had a shit-fit on the way home so everyone nearly puked. The black lady who'd made her oatmeal every morning at Cow Jumped Over the Moon daycare. How she'd fed the calves sugar in the palm of her hand. Her first Halloween dressed as a moocow, six houses over in Dover, she'd been afraid to ring the doorbell. A man whose little girl had been killed bit Daddy's finger off and swallowed it. *Swallowed it!* he'd always say, as if the act remained beyond belief.

They'd flown to Little Rock once, after, for his grandpa's 100th birthday, though he was long dead, and driven to the house, two big pastures with a barn rising behind the house. The driveway was long as a football field, a well-house in the wooded front yard. Two roadrunners, a hen and cock, had trotted by while they idled out on the gravel road, a woman standing way off behind the storm door of where they used to live, staring at them. Someone had built a play station. There had been children. A kite was caught in the limbs of the tallest hickory. Where she would have grown up. Could have.

Didn't.

Her last memory is of hunting Easter eggs in the huge back-yard with her cousins, grown with kids now. She would have had a southern accent, say she had to go *tee-tee*, know how to skin squirrels and make snow cream. It had snowed hard once and there's a photo of her on the deck wearing ski goggles, her face lifted to the falling flakes as if her body knew that it had snowed on the morning she was born that January in Utah. Where they'd go, Daddy and Dozo in the Hertz-Penske, her and Mom in the Pathfinder. Up through Missouri to Nebraska, the Ogallala trail along the South Platte into Wyoming. Earth rose up into mountains, the backbone of the continent where water reversed its course and rolled west through the great gorges to the Pacific.

The old way.

The way Daddy's people had walked, down the west slope of the Uintas to Emigration Canyon and south toward California. Only the Mormons had dressed as Indians and killed them all save the babies, left them laying for wolves to eat near a place called New Harmony. The single worst massacre of all Manifest Destiny. She'd heard it enough that it had lost its meaning. Growing up in Utah, where her soccer teammates wouldn't eat the jumbo extra special strawberries she brought for game snack, how they talked about the sleepovers they were having that night, or how cool it was they were going to the Jonas Brothers Concert next Tuesday. Pretending to be Mormon and getting caught. Filth. Written in pink fingernail polish on her East High locker.

Florida had been a blessing, despite what sent them there.

At the Atkins Exit, two giant signs dominate the hillside. One is a Razorback Hog, *Woo Pig Sooie* written under its hooves. The other, DON'T YOU MAKE ME COME DOWN THERE, 1st Atkins Church of God. Taken together, the message riddled her, Reverend Jodie Love's gospel blues coming in loud and clear past Alma to Fort Smith and the vast green Choctaw land beyond.

On her grandmother's side, Lucy Harvell's, she was a Jenkins, who were cousins to the Youngers, who'd ridden with the James Gang after the War Between the States when the carpetbaggers came down into Dixie to steal whatever hadn't already been stolen. Mom Dee's brother was named Tom Howard, Mr. Jessie James' alias when he was shot in the back by Bob Ford on a spring night, what you get when you grow up with a history professor father, who'd left Arkansas physically, but never in his heart. Outlaw in her blood, along with dwarf and Cherokee and pirate from Mom's side, Captain John Hawkins, thank you. She'd refused the twelve-gauge shotgun with the box of shiny green shells; who goes driving across country with a gun like that? But she'd brought the lockblade Buck hunter, on her belt that second, sharp as it was the day he gave it to her.

He'd lost the one O.W. had given him, in the Green River down on Desolation, and took it as a sign for things to come. Sure enough, he'd fallen off the ladder that very fall, wrapping plastic around the swamp cooler just outside the kitchen window. He'd asked her to help him, and she had because Mom said to. A sixty-year-old man up on a ladder like that. "Hold it. Don't let him fall," she'd said.

But he broke the rules. Had always broken the rules. A silver plate was welded on the top rung, red letters saying DO NOT STAND. And of course he stood right on top of it, reached to pull a sheet of plastic across, a strip of duct tape between his teeth. October 19th, and he'd always said that nineteen was his unlucky number, how old his brother was for the car wreck, driving Highway 319, leery of nineteens for the rest of his life, save that afternoon, when the light had that gold tint to it, and snow had already fallen up on the Wasatch, a nip in the air, game one of the World Series that night, lamb curry simmering on the stove. You could smell it through the cooler, the curry, and he'd reached too deep across the top of the suspended window box, let it hold his weight. Wedged over the window-sill into the opening, he'd framed the cooler in before she was born, had wrapped it twenty times against winter since. Year in, year out, he'd leave sage inside, there was no way it was going anywhere, their swamp.

Until it did.

The fall took forever, that look on his face. Disbelief. A question. She'd turned loose and jumped away at the last second, or the thing would have crushed her, too.

He'd tried to talk, to say something.

Mom heard from inside. She was screaming into the phone. And when the ambulance slammed up in front of their house, she realized that it was a Saturday, a game day, and about thirty thousand Ute fans had started streaming up their street to the stadium, and now the EMTs were having to dodge them with the silver gurney, how strange.

They'd cut his shirt off, a new flannel, and Daddy'd said *no*.

At the ER, they could hear him screaming from the waiting room, *a good thing*, the woman they'd sent out to keep them from losing their minds said. When she'd tried to visit him in ICU, the elevator had gotten stuck for a full ten minutes, so she was crying when he looked up at her from underneath the pain meds. "I'm okay, I'm okay," he'd said.

But the elevator had shaken her, and she couldn't stay. First night of the World Series, they'd watched it together since she was a kid, yelled at the batters, chattered between plays, bet each other household chores on the outcome of a given game. Who was even playing that year?

October 19, 2019, a Saturday. Game day. The crowd up the street thundering in the stands. *We must protect this house*, she remembered them chanting. *We must protect this house*.

First night of the series. Eating cold curry with Mom.

She gassed at Shawnee, hit the girl's room, and when she got back to the car, a man stood at the passenger side, looking in the window. He saw her unsnap the knife case on her right hip, shook his head and walked away into the growing dark. She was tired.

Lucy should gauge her tires. That's what he'd say. The right front looks low, you should check it.

Tomorrow.

Never do tomorrow what you can do today.

She carried the guitar into the hotel room, 102, the page number of "The Three Pigs" in *Treasury of Literature for Children: A Collection of the Best-Loved Classic Stories and Rhymes*.

"Page 102," she'd say at bedtime when asked what she

wanted to read. Whatever happened to that book, they'd thrown away so much for the move. She laid it across the bed, unsnapped the silver buckles and opened the case, took the instrument into her hands. It had a smell to it, fresh and clean, the spruce top meeting rosewood up the high frets, mother of pearl inlay, neck straight as a string. A D-28, it was the same guitar Hank Williams played, the one Neil Young somehow bought, so the sound was true and recognizable across space and time. What he'd said, across space and time.

Outside, the waning moon rises over Oklahoma. It would shine on the surf at Melbourne Beach where this all started, where Mom walked some nights checking for sea turtles crawled up in the dunes to lay eggs. Make sure nothing bothered them, dogs, raccoons, skunks sometimes.

She knew one song, exactly. She strums E-minor, six times, and then to the D, a bright chord after the minor's dark. It would shine down on the woolly-headed Washers in Arizona, on Mr. Paris in Dinnehotso, the full Flower Moon.

This near the highway, Lucy hears the diesels gearing up and down from the Shawnee Exit, just off 70.

He'd had a horse named that once, Shawnee. Was that why she'd stopped here, because of Daddy's horse, the hunk of red mustang hair he'd kept in the ceramic turtle?

The pizza man knocks, says, "102?"

And just like that, she's laughing. *Not by the hair of my chinny-chin-chin, I'll not let you in.*

He looked at her funny, making change.

"It's Three Pigs," she said, the box hot on her fingertips.

She saw him see the guitar on the bed, then pretend he hadn't.

"Thank you."

"You too."

The bolt clicks when she locks it. She does the latch. He'd forgot the red pepper, the pizza man, but the parmesan was there, salt and pepper. Little folded napkin with a plastic spoon and knife.

2.

For a long time Officer Roger D. Stoner had wondered at what happened on the pedestrian twin of Navajo bridge, the one originally named for his great grandfather, John Doyle Lee, how he'd smelled rat and tracked the Arkies there, although exactly what they were up to had alluded him. For a while, it had. Some beef with Mormons, no doubt, and the fact that he'd imprisoned the skinny one at Coconino County for indecent exposure and vandalism on federal land, urinating in public and defamation of distinguished persons as manifest at heritage sites, not to mention slander and assault on an officer of the peace. Sixty days in, and that many again on probation with the Harvell punk up in Salt Lake, violated sure as shit. So said the bench warrant from the Old World out in the snow-covered cruiser, doors still frozen shut, likely.

Jacob's Lake, on the North Rim of the Grand Canyon, was two things most all of the time: cold and lonely. A deep-dark-brooding kind of lonely that makes him wish he hadn't burned up the last of her letters, Joanna's. That he could warm himself with her words, even if they had a cold edge to them. He'd got rid of everything she'd ever touched, except himself, and with the plague and aloneness the way it has been up until recently, that had been on the table, too. Sure it had. Him having to patrol Navajo land, when they had the virus about twenty times

14

worse than New York City, where refrigerated semi-trucks lined up outside all the hospitals, about to haul the dead over to this island they'd turned into a mass grave. Only they had access to clean water for handwashing, folk up in New York City. Down here, on the Rez, wasn't water to drink, much less wash your hands. People'd died left and right, curfew'd been on since who knows when, everything shut down, everything.

The vaccines had made their way in March and April, Stoner'd taken both in the left shoulder, and hadn't got sick, though Elder Kavapulu who managed the Inn had got the chills for two days straight, same for his wife, so he'd had to man the front office, Stoner.

And out here, seemed like there were two kinds: white folk who believed the virus was a hoax perpetrated by liberals to steal the election from their idiot president, and anti-vaxxers. Both stupid as sacksful of hammers.

Word was they'd open the park this summer, unmasked. The Navajo Nation had floated opening to non-Indians again, so the San Juan would put river left back on the table, Chinle Wash, Canyon de Chelly. They could crawl out of the funk they'd lived in going on fourteen months. And things ought to get interesting then, huh? Everyone living in curfew and lock-down set free of their stinking hibernation, let their hair down and get into some trouble. Just the sort of mess Stoner was looking for. Bring it on.

The radio beside the kitchen sink monkey-chatters. Snow glares on the mesa. The trailer stinks—smells like him. Stoner opened a window and breathed in a fresh cold air, with a cut of spruce in it, wood fire from the Inn. The birds were at it, fox squirrels emboldened from the lack of humans, gone missing one whole season now.

He knew men on the force up to Vernal, but he'd resisted having them run Joanna's name. Living with her father probably still, head warlock in the temple there, all the redneck miners driving new trucks, and their kid's teeth rotting out from meth. He'd resisted checking up on her. Had she been vaccinated? Was she okay? *Jo?*

Would it be so wrong?

Time to crawl out of his hole. Thaw out the car and make the circuit. Drive on over to Tuba City, give Monument Valley a whirl. News was the Arkie was living with Indians there, the Begays who for some reason saw fit to let him court Rose Marie, who'd been Miss University of Utah Native American once, and could certainly do better than that buck-toothed beaver. They'd been up to something, the Arkies at the bridge.

The warrant for Paris had expired. He'd have it renewed. Reinstate the fucker. Soon as he was better, he would.

Everything she'd ever touched but himself he'd got rid of. Not exactly true, was it. There was the earth she'd walked on, what about that? In Page, their home, overlooking the beginning of the Grand Fucking Canyon, what she'd say, preacher's daughter, that glint in her eye. Brother'd Temple married them in Salt Lake, and she'd badgered him all the way south to tell her the secret name, the one he'd call out at the end of time so they could inhabit their own planet, him and Joanna, and whatever other wives and offspring were sealed to Stoner's eternal being.

So that first night in the house had been stony, if not the next few. He didn't make the rules. It was part of it. And it was a funny word, the magic name, wasn't it? One that stuck on the tongue. He was not to ever say it, her holy name, not till the end of time. Which the plague sort of seemed like, circling over the world, killing rich and poor, white and colored, Jew, Christian and Indian alike. Was now the time?

The first time he said it was in a dream.

She'd come to him, he smelled her breath, the *crème de menthe* sweet and warm on his neck, the indent in the mattress where she once lay, and he'd woke himself up saying it, Jo's holy name.

A suspect had been apprehended at mile marker 32 outside Kayenta, awaiting backup, surveilling from a distance, unmasked, right brake light out, Armadillo-Rooster-something plates, too muddy to tell. The radio goes in and out. Sometimes he half expects her voice to come out of it. How Joanna'd get to talking, moving her hands and gesticulating, so the story'd come alive, whatever she was telling, say the time she and a girlfriend stole her daddy's car and drove down to Dinosaur and swam naked at the take-out, and a Ranger'd caught them and offered chase, and she'd fallen out of the car and butt-skidded on the gravel road. It was still embedded in the left cheek, gravel.

"I won't come," she'd said that last night. "You call me all you want. I won't come."

Like all their other fights, it wasn't really about what it was about. She'd sprayed hairspray in the bathroom because she knew it made him sick to his stomach, or wrapped the front hose around the handrail because she knew it didn't go there, or moved the couch away from the wall so the coffee table blocked the fireplace—she knew how to get his goat. Did she ever.

"You won't have a choice," he said. Supper time, everything about to explode. They could have stopped right there. But they didn't.

"The hell I won't."

The plates didn't match the vehicle, the suspect's, a dead giveaway. Male and female, looks like an Indian. Pickup with a camper, heading north toward Monument Pass. All those Indians out there on the Rez swapped plates, request for pursuit denied. DMF 936—there was no such plate issued in Arizona. What gives?

She'd squared her shoulders, stood to her full height. Made both hands into fists. Supper time, but no supper. The radio on, monkey chattering. Time going slow-mo the way it did sometimes. They'd said the things that crossed the line, worse. And next day, Jo was gone, and the day after that and the next. No phone calls, no nothing. Except the note, the one he'd burned in the fireplace and threw the ashes off the gorge into the canyon, packed up and moved to the trailer at Jacob's Lake, and then came the plague dragging its shed skin of sadness, and this.

He could run her name, find out where she lived. In a good way. They needed to talk. One way or the other, they needed at least that. People who stayed mad at each other still loved each other. You could only love what you could hate. Hadn't he read that somewhere, Stoner? Had his mother told him such? One road from Mexican Water all the way to Vernal, Highway 191, seven, eight hours one way.

The Green River's up there, Flaming Gorge Dam, and the primo trout fishing down through Swallow Canyon into Colorado. They could fish-float it, camp the primitive sites, eat fresh trout and listen to coyotes yip-yap off the eastern slopes of the High Uintas. If he could talk her into it, if they could make up, if that wasn't too much.

May Day, the world was coming back. He breathed it in, Stoner, smelled eggs and bacon, good hashbrowns from the Inn. People'd started coming back—the worst of it had passed. He'd shave, put on clean clothes and get on with his life. What else? The snow was melting, glacier lilies blooming soon, hills rife with sunflower, Mule Ear and Balsam Root. Scarlet Gilia.

He'd talk to Kavapulu and eat breakfast, black coffee and a morning paper. The fire would snap, crackle and pop and the sun would warm his face through the plate glass. He'd write her a letter, that's what he'd do. Once he had the address, he would. Say the things that needed to be said. Make his offer, his peace. It was the right thing to do, surely it was.

Outside that second, a raven caw-cawed. She could make that sound exactly, Jo could. So it was a sign telling him he was on the right track, the raven's voice. He'd heard one that could say *help!*, a raven. Had tricked a group of hikers into leaving their packs unprotected, then doubled back and opened them with beak and claw, hog-gobbled all their freeze-dried lasagna, so they had to live on a pack of peanuts and some Hersey's kisses until they got out. Maybe that's what this was, her calling *help*.

Mud-spattered, it wasn't Arizona at all. DMF 936, an Arkansas plate. Edgar T. Paris. Sixty days then probation from Coconino County. Release, September 2018 to Joey Harvell. Negative on the pursuit, about to cross the state line.

Heading for it.

Black against the fierce white snow, the raven flew, its voice the exact tenor as hers.

3.

The name of the cave was Big Cave One, BC[1] for short, and the story went that this anthropologist named Kidding had dug up a teenage mother with her baby tied to a cradle board from a Basket Maker burial cist up there. A thousand years old, maybe two. Now *Viva Las Vegas* is spray-painted above the entrance, which Rose pointed out from the house-size boulder where they parked. He wished he didn't know that, about the mother and baby. Cold outside, they sipped coffee in the truck cab that smelled of fry bread and corn pollen, the sky-blue bundle Big Rose sent with them as spirit offering. The world had got so big on Edgar, sandstone fins tall as skyscrapers rise from the land from here to there, sky like a blue bowl flipped over them, a different color blue than any in Arkansas or anywhere else, like blue from the flipping moon or something. Makes him dizzy to look at it—this sky. Monument Valley. These *Diné* had another name for it, one that caught on their tongues, the way old man Titsworth's had back at Dover Church of God, hard words that resisted their saying. Big Rose had taught him one to say before going in the cave.

"What for?" he asked.

The old woman had smiled, punched his shoulder with her left hand. Didn't answer. She'd taught Rose some words as well. Sounds from the moon coming out her mouth. Hissing over where she missed a tooth.

An extra fry-biscuit sat wrapped in foil on the dash, buttered, defrost warmed. A trick his daddy who was a long-haul trucker had taught him before making that last long deadhead to meet his maker. A Sunday morning, a hundred and forty sticks of TNT in the bed behind them, a medicine bundle and bread, words. BC[1] up there with its black mouth yawning. *Viva las Vegas.*

He practiced saying it, his word.

Rose said, "Roll your window down, let it out."

"The word?"

She opened the door, got out, so a whiff of it caught him.

"Oh, sorry."

She wore her hair down her back, Rose Begay. She had a good laugh, which she was laughing that second. "Tell me what it means, Big Rose," she teased, her voice sing-song.

Who'd of thought this bone-chilling cold in the desert? "Well what does it mean? Is it a mojo?"

She had a flashlight she was flipping on and off, the big kind truckers use to check their tires in the dark, enough to whomp Jesus out of somebody if they messed with you.

She raised both shoulders, dropped them. "Just say it. Can't hurt."

"Best save that light."

She shined it in his face, so a little white dot twinkled behind his eyelids when he closed them. The rock that was big as a house was named House Rock. "That's House Rock," Rose said. Horned animals were pecked into syrupy patina, the silhouette of a spray-painted hand, some beer cans and an old car battery. Catching light already.

She stepped on the goat trail that zig-zagged up to where they were going. "You sure you want to do this Edgar?"

Was anybody ever sure about anything? "Yeah," he said. "I guess."

He followed. She wore pink pants. *Peach*, she'd corrected him. Looked like a teacher, which she was.

"Do better than I guess."

"The Russians won't take it back. 'It's shit,' they said. Harvell's gone. Not safe, no way in hell at Big Rose's. She said it's a good place. You ever been here?"

So quiet, just thundering bygod quiet. He'd never get used to it, Edgar.

Her shoes had heels. Who climbed in heels?

"On a dare," Rose said. "Look."

Where she pointed was a far-off fin, orange-colored in the morning light. A hand of spires, fingers to the sky, the tips of each crowned in alpenglow. Something black sailed across a highway invisible on the horizon, a faint flash and then it was gone.

"Valley of the Gods," Rose said. "I'll take you there sometime."

The hand lifting its fingers skyward was a sign for something to come, marked the end of one thing and the beginning of another, somehow. White folk called it The Seven Sailors, but the Navajo said the individual spires were warrior spirits that kept an eye on Bears Ears—holy land, the Garden of Eden for a whole slew of tribes, Edgar'd learn. But for now, it rose out there like an Egyptian pyramid or something. A backdrop to a John Wayne movie. A place where holy men went to pray.

Just then light struck the cave mouth. "Don't forget the bundle. And the biscuit." She said the words that Big Rose had taught her and disappeared beneath the overhang.

Just like that, the light darting.

He'd ever follow her, Rose. Had hallucinated her before they ever met, even back on the Navajo Bridge when Stoner'd whacked him for pissing on the bronze of John Doyle Lee, his great, great grandfather or something, *a man of indomitable courage and sound judgement*. Fucker. Who'd executed one hundred forty some of Edgar's kin whose names are written one by one on the sticks of TNT in the liquor store boxes in his camper that second, the one's he'd had to chisel from the sandstone underbelly of the bridge, lest the thing go off and hurt somebody didn't deserve it. The Harvell boy'd got cold feet at the last second, walked away from it like nobody'd ever know. How they'd planned to blow the bridge named for John Doyle Lee, maybe take its twin down with it. What had got it all started, him walking out on the bridge with the godawful bird big as a dinosaur roosted on a brace, number four spray painted on a ten foot wing. How he'd turned a corner and seen the bronze, ten feet tall, fat man's godson doing the fat man's business. *Avenging the prophet*, what they said. Well hell with that, Edgar'd pulled down and splattered the thing, only the officer had snuck up behind him, whacked him from behind with the billy stick. Wasn't that just like the Mormons, whack you from behind?

Edgar'd hallucinated the Navajo girl, the Indian princess of the western world, wearing her wealth of turquoise and porcupine quill, her turtle amulet whipping in the wind, borne up on the wings of the mutant angel-bird, the fierce white cross zigzagged on its underside. She'd beckoned for him to follow, did Rose Marie Begay. The great speckled bird lifted them to the place, whatever they chose to name it in the human tongue. No words, finally, for that destination, that way of being, where future and past twine.

"You coming, Edgar?"

"I'm right behind you," he said, but truth was he didn't want to go in, there was something about the story of that teenage mother and her baby the archeologists had dug up from a thousand years ago or something. She'd been buried with a full human head scalp tied around her neck, Big Rose said, the hair combed out perfectly and bobbed, a green stripe painted across the face. Strong medicine, for a long time no Indian would touch Big Cave One with a ten-foot pole. Nobody. People'd spit when they drove past, Big Rose said. Then some kids took to spray-painting inside and out, so now the place was sort of a graffiti house of horrors—sex, death and heavy metal on every nook and cranny. Opening to the north, the burial cave is cold inside. It's the right thing to do, Big Rose said, interring the dynamite there, each of the named sticks from the massacre.

It made sense.

He retrieved the medicine bundle, the biscuit. A water bottle. Something told him to run like hell, but of course he wouldn't do that. The stone fin out there lifting fingers to the great blue sky, a big world getting bigger so that Edgar's thin shadow is diminished, nothing at all by the time he crawls into the mouth of BC¹.

4.

One true thing about driving west is that the road empties out by daylight, and you can see forever, and Luce discovers that she can hold her breath from one mile marker to the next, sixty seconds, a mile a minute. Outside Shamrock, she tried it on a whim, nothing on the radio, all the blow by truckers asleep in their cabs at the Rest Stop. Today, she'd hit New Mexico, Tucumcari, the name of the town in that song he liked—*give me weed, whites and wine, show me a sign, and I'll be willing to be moving.* The numbers are getting smaller, 87 to 86 in one breath, only a little dizzy. At the exits sometimes stands a hitchhiker, and there was a part of her that would have enjoyed the talk, the stories—everyone had a story, didn't they? What were we but the stories that twisted through our time on earth, for her going on twenty-five years now, her schools, her teachers, soccer for a while, that runaway road trip with Jack down to Tucson to meet her dwarf Uncle Davey, and make peace with that side of his family Daddy'd never meet.

She sees the green mile markers about the time the breath starts to burn in her chest. The first time she blacked out was a surprise, opening eyes and registering she'd been out, that she'd lost consciousness. The implications. The second time, that other-worldly feel of driving through a place you've never been and really weren't at now, scared her. Noon, outside Amarillo, with its hot, dry May Day winds. Lucy hits a rest area and finds a covered picnic table, hauls her cooler to shade. A woman walks a yellow dog around the perimeter, talking to it just like it was talking back, answering questions, mapping out the afternoon to come. The breathing game was silly, best get a dog and talk to it cross country, let it explain why exactly they were doing what they were doing. Right?

The pizza box has absorbed some ice melt, not bad. Vegi-supreme, the bell peppers remind her of a sign at the end of their street summer before last. LOST, it had said, PET HAMSTER. DOESN'T BITE. LOVES BELL PEPPERS. REWARD.

Underneath, a picture of the thing, with the caption, "I'm lonely."

And of course, like a fool, she'd called the number and it was all a scam, some guy who tried to sell her weed over the phone, and kept calling her back until she had the number blocked. He told her he had a new hamster, Scout, and this one was crazy for arugula. Would she like to come over and meet him, little munchie Scout?

The lemonade is cold, hits the spot. She smells like hotel soap, Luce, the shampoo and conditioner. Mom had promised to stop tracking her every mile. The heat had come on at Melbourne Beach, a transport ship big as an island had lost a platform of Tequila, so everyone and their mother was down in the surf, hauling out the bounty. Drinking straight from the bottle. Was she okay? At the cemetery, had it been hard? Did she wish her mother there for it? Was she sure she wanted to keep going? The guitar stuff. She'd feel better if there was a friend along.

What friend?

You know, Mom'd said. *Someone.*

She'd slipped chocolate into the cooler. A ziploc stuffed with caramels. Good after the salty pizza.

In the bathroom she had a panic attack that she'd forgot to lock the car, but when she got out everything was okay, the shape of the black case under the beach towel Salt Lake School District had given Mom for her retirement, her name in blue cursive on one side, but not the other. Nearly twenty-five years, same age as her, same as when Mom met dad in Fayetteville that spring time, when she was on spring break from her Arlington teaching job and had flown down to meet her pen pal on an Easter Sunday that corresponded with April Fool's that year.

Where her story begins, the two of them meeting.

What would she do if someone took it? The instrument. Would insurance cover it? Was it even possible to replace a 1998 Martin D-28 with a Fishman Transducer pickup? *Don't give it to a boyfriend.*

He'd lost a guitar once. She'd heard the story, the history of the thing. An Ovation, Anniversary Edition, he'd borrowed money from a girl and let her keep the guitar until he could pay her back. And he'd hit on the last race at Oaklawn one day, only the girl he was with was tipsy and he'd had to drive, and rear-ended somebody on the way out of Hot Springs. She'd made him use the money he'd won on the deductible and he never saw the guitar again. Story was he'd taught an extra class when Mom was pregnant, picked the Martin out at Intermountain Guitar and Banjo, and paid on it with every paycheck, until it was clear. He'd played it for her those mornings when Mom had gone back to work and his belt buckle left little dents in the body and she remembered the sound of his voice to the notes. In middle school, they'd played a duet of Pachelbel's Canon in D, at the Episcopalian Church, him on guitar and her on piano, Mom's bright face out there, and somebody laughed and said it was a wedding song, which it sort of was, but pretty.

The front passenger tire blows just over the state line, mile marker 372. She should have gauged it, the tool that second in her center console. *Welcome to New Mexico* a sign that bridged I-40 one side to the other said, *Land of Enchantment.* A welcome center rest stop was right over there, surely it wouldn't hurt to drive that far.

Luce thump-thumped into the lot, parked square between yellow lines. She could smell it now that the windows were down, a jolt of adrenalin vibrating up her forearms. She'd once slid into a curb near the dorms in a snowstorm when her dad was teaching nearby at Officer's Circle. He'd called class early and driven her over, jacked the thing up and had the lugnuts off just like that. She remembered how he lay on his back in the snow to get the jack just right.

Luce could change a tire, he'd taught her that much.

5.

State Road 160 is the exact place where Stoner had to decide to head North and East though Tuba City and on to Monument Valley where the Arkie was no doubt up to no good, or south to Flag and the Coconino County Seat to formally reinstate Bench Warrant 666071 in the name of Edgar Trent Paris who violated probation in December 2018 in the vicinity of Navajo Bridge, which Stoner was just then passing over, the green Colorado with that May glow about it before the monsoons came and turned it to shit. Scene of the original crime, it still got his goat, didn't it, pissing on a government monument. If he headed north, he'd be moving toward Joanna, and the very highway, 191, which rolled up to Vernal City with its dumb-dumb Dino-land Park a stone's throw from the Temple. He knew she was there, the apartment number, and had even been gifted a working phone number should he wish to dial it. And her warlock daddy could just go jump in the lake, couldn't he? Brother, too. It had been tough, the black plague. On everybody. Wearing the masks, washing the skin off your hands, the virus run through the jailhouse like a bat out of hell—best stay away from there, and he had, hadn't he? Just as bad in St. George, ignorant bastards. COVID-19 was not a hoax invented by liberals to throw the election, though they would have if they could have. Nor was the vaccine the work of Satan to brainwash their kids, though they'd have liked that too, brainwashing the kids. It was the real deal, this virus, he'd seen it with his own eyes.

The Indians got it worst. Look what happened to Chief Joseph, pouring water over the hot rocks in that sweat lodge, everybody in there sucking it into their lungs. So the whole place went on lockdown quarantine. He'd just about had enough of that, Stoner. Jacob's Lake on the North Rim sat square atop no man's land, and the son of a bitch bug somehow managed to fly there too, nearly killed Elder Kavapulu, and then his wife, so maybe the PCIs had the same blood in them as Indians. Who knew?

The vaccinations had come like the cavalry, except that was all a bunch of baloney, wasn't it, the stuff about the cavalry riding to the rescue. Truth was, it was men in blue like himself did the saving—blue lives matter, fucking A.

Over there on the pedestrian side sits Rita Begay. Folding silver wire around feathers, making her mojos like she ever had. It was her daughter, Rose Marie, taken up with the very Arkie in question, though how that had come to be, Stoner doesn't yet know. But he'll find out, won't he? Just pull on over to the parking lot of the PED bridge, have a word.

No law against that, huh?

May 2nd, a Sunday morning, bright and shiny. She'd burned cedar. Under the authentic Navajo limb-covered shelter, he could smell it.

The air's fresh. He'd showered and shaved, clipped his nails. Packed a clean change of clothes and extra box of number one buck for the twelve gauge. A couple ham sammies from Mrs. Kavapulu back at the Inn on ice in the cooler, the imprint of where he'd once worn a wedding band indelible on his left ring finger.

"Morning, Rita," he said.

She nodded, Begay, looked at her fingers, how they braided the silver wire around a tiny hoop laced with green feathers. A whole table of them set up as tourist bait. It was said that not to buy one in passing was bad luck, that was the word, spread by Indians, no doubt, likely, raking it in for hoops and feathers.

"How you been?"

Rita nodded three times, worked the wire. She was wearing tennis shoes, he knows without looking, she always wore tennis shoes, a skirt and shawl, sometimes a smart-alecky t-shirt said something like HOMELAND SECURITY under a picture of Geronimo and Cochise and some other Indians with rifles. Did she know they weren't even Navajo?

How you talk to Indians. Smoke signals.

"I'm wondering. How's ole Rose doing? She still teaching over to the Monument?"

Rita nodded, smiled. Under the table was a .357 magnum Lynyrd'd named *Koyanisqatsi*, Kuya for short, because that's the name her grandfather, who was called Sun Bear, had given this bridge at the naming ceremony, after it was decided that it could not be called John Doyle Lee Bridge. He was a medicine chief, Sun Bear, and the whites just ate that Indian shit up. *Yeah, call it Koyanisqatsi*, though of course no one knew jack about what it meant, the name the elder Begay gave his white brothers as the right word.

World out of balance. Sure enough.

He's giving her his white mansplaining look, dumb Rez Indian, folding trinkets for Germans. Lynyrd'd written names on all the bullets with a red sharpie—what else did he have to do, wash dishes for the river rats to eat off over at Marble Canyon Lodge, drink his PBR, maybe run the river for swamper money if a party needed somebody. Probably one of them had Stoner's name on it in the—what was it called, the thing that revolved where you put the shells in little holes—right this second. What would he think about that, Jack? Kuya boy's business end pointed straight up at his hoo-hoos? She felt the heat on her face, held onto the smile.

They believed their boogey-man medicine could turn

Indians white. It was actually written in their book, their holy doctrine of covenants, the one that named her a Lamanite and said her and Big Rose's skin tone was a curse from their god for being unrighteous—what a load of hooey. What'd he been smoking, Joseph Smith?

Of course, he was here to find out about Birdy. They weren't allowed to work on Sunday, were they. And if you told them that the book said they had to tell the truth when asked to do so, they weren't allowed to lie. Blah, blah, blah.

She'd not minded about Rose and Edgar. He had some sense about him, and something had happened down in Flag in Chief Joseph's sweat lodge, he'd taken to white sage and cedar, stretched a deerskin drum, and wrote his prayer around the wood frame. Learned some songs, even. He made Big Rose laugh, and that was much better than the other. Sure it was. Lynyrd had taught him to make fry bread for the tacos tourist went ga-ga for. He was good with a shovel, even in rock. Could work with tools. She could have done worse, Rose.

The way the boys around here'd become hooligans, spray-painting everything and its mother, going maskless, skipping powwow and drum circle and pinyon nut gatherings—which, to tell the truth, were not Rita's favorite either, but still. They were messed up, kids today. Had they always been?

Rose had come back to teach, but she wouldn't stay. No one stayed. Why would they? People like John Stoner there in front of her face giving them shit all the time. She touched her right knee to Kuya—cool beneath the table.

"No school on Sunday," Rose said. She let the smile loose, just a little.

Stoner nodded, twitched his shoulders up and down.

She hadn't gotten it, the sickness. First had been Lynyrd, then Big Rose, went through the whole house just like that. Hit Birdy hardest, him all shivering under three blankets, making those whistle noises. All behind them now, all of that.

She's had the medicine, Big Rose and little, Lynyrd and Bird. Just about the whole nation by now. Until the next sickness got passed their way again, like the time before that and the time before that.

Out on the high point of the PED, a condor shakes off its wings, bright number 7 spray painted on one wing. Harvey she calls that one. Good morning, Harvey. Stoner turned to see what she was looking at, holds a hand above his eye in salute to the bird.

"Reckon not," he said.

Stoner picked up a hummingbird mojo, turned it over in his fingers. One of her spirit totems, little gladiator. She'd seen them fly up in the face of eagles, just levitate there, eye to eye.

"Guess I'll take this one," he said, dug out his wallet, handed her a five. "Tell'em I say hi, her and that Arky."

She hands him two ones and a fifty cent piece, says, "Half price on Sunday."

6.

Used to be no one would go there in a million-gazillion years, the burial cist where they'd found the girl and her baby, a human scalp tied round her neck with the hair bobbed perfect. A green stripe painted across the face. The sort of medicine that could work its way into you and never leave. She'd known a man once who carried a human jawbone, set it atop anything he didn't want stolen. Indian insurance—used to work that way. But not anymore, no. Nowadays, nothing was out of bounds, not even cold north-facing Big Cave One. She'd been wrong to send them there with it, hadn't she. Despite what the prayer dream had told her, she'd been wrong. Hadn't she, Big Rose?

Some of those kids could get hurt. Bad hurt. That Yazzie one who was leading the rest, blasting "Highway to Hell" out his broken car speakers. Flipping the bird to anyone said anything. Smoking tooth-rot medicine. She'd not seen it coming, this generation, dead set on being the last.

They'd have to go back and disinter them, those names Mormons claimed Indians killed all those years ago, when Sun Bear was a boy even, and had watched the massacre from a hilltop north and west of here.

Koyanisqatsi, they called it, world out of balance.

It was the first thing she'd thought of when Bird-Man told

them what they'd done, how him and the college professor had drilled holes under the bridge her grandfather had named, though now they just called it Navajo Bridge, both of them as if they were one, had written the names of each dead on the sticks, cemented them in and wired it to blow. And something had happened there at the end, at the last moment, that changed their minds, so they left it be, until Edgar had gone and chiseled them out, all one hundred and forty.

It made perfect sense—taking them to BC[1]. And then the dream came, and she knew. But maybe it was just a dream. Maybe it was.

These smarty pants who knew it all anthropologists—peachy faces, Lynyrd'd call them—dug up the child bride with her baby, that painted scalp around her neck, some nerve not to leave them be. Disturbed the medicine, fucked with the balance. She'd done it herself, once, Big Rose, fucked with the balance. Back then you could drive any old junker over Black Mesa into Butler Wash, make for the Butt Formation turnoff, get out and walk through the gap-toothed barbed wire, faint trail north to the big cedar with the rockwork irrigation system from the sweetwater spring bubbling up. A good lookout point above, you could see fifty miles to the Aneth gas fields and the dirty San Juan. She'd run away from home, sort of, way back when. In a stripped down car she'd maybe stolen, just for a week or so. She needed to find out who she was, who she was going to be, and how to manifest such a person without losing her everloving mind. Grandfather Sun Bear had died, there'd been that shit at Pine Ridge, the movement, all that. But mostly, just the same ole same ole. Nothing, nothing, and more nothing, shaking, making the rounds. Anyway, she'd left for a while. Drove to the place Sunny B had once told her about, when she was a girl and prone to believe.

It was a holy place. She was to make an offering. Tobacco, something living. Seek the Butt Formation. Walk the thin path north. Look for the big cedar. Been there five hundred years. Say prayer. Make the old words. Leave what didn't serve her behind.

She'd done it just the way he said. Brought the offering, made the words. Found the place by accident, it was invisible, just like he said. Existed in a time and space where a seam had been made between then and now, and you could walk right through, but you had to be careful. That's what he'd said, Sunny B, you had to be careful because the spirits watched you, and they could swallow you up and shit you out in two seconds flat. Watch your ass.

It had been in summer, the chokecherries not yet ripe. Windless, still.

Stepped into the canopy of cedar shade, the shadow exploding upward, a rush palpable in the still air, so she thought she'd have a heart attack and die there at the mouth of the village hidden inside the seam of time. The great owl's shadow wings fell on her, and it was cold-cold, too close to night.

Bear, wolf, eagle, antelope. Hawk. Fish. The great horned owl had flown up on speckled wings. Her vision at the Butt Formation over in Butler Wash, when she'd walked to the cedar and the land unfolded itself to her and she could see—the painted kiva and water works, the birthing stone and place of naming, the lookout where pottery was made, a stone for skinning, metate for grinding. When the afternoon sun went golden and she found her way, and then she didn't. A piece of green glass, worn smooth, lay on the altar, and the great blind spot in Big Rose saw it as trash, litter left by those ignorant of all that mattered in this world. Who'd haul down and shit in your church, defile the house of the falling rain.

Trash from the world outside, that's how she saw it, Big Rose, there at the altar of time and space. A piece of green bottle glass, worn smooth, laid at the foot of where holy ones had stood, maybe blood kin from beyond the memories of Sun Bear even, all the way back to the ones who'd hunted and fished their way across the land bridge, walked down to the Columbia River Gorge and turned right at the Snake, took aim on the Salmon and the sweetwater that ran down to the confluence and beyond. Here they'd wailed and died and loved, made children and worshipped Corn Maiden with yellow pollen, snake danced and cherished all that was alive and living. The green of growing things, mother of life, mother of death.

And in her great blind spot she'd seen the worn smooth green glass as trash and swiped it up with a hand, thrust it into a pocket with righteous indignation, forgive them, father, they know not what they do.

She took the glass, river smoothed, the green of growing things.

And at that moment, the great horned owl who'd laid it there burst up through the shade of cedar, screaming and flap-flapping so she thought she'd die that second, but did not make the connection, not yet. A hard wind blew up and she was scared. The place shut itself off from her. She walked back through barbed wire, the Butt Formation to her right, where a sign would one day say do not touch the ancient artifacts under penalty of jail time and fine.

She'd driven ten yards when the back tire blew out, passenger side. The wind came on then, fierce, nearly blew the door off when she opened it, fumbling for the jack in the trunk, the spare. The four-way. And when she lay on her back to set the hoist under a piece of frame, the sudden pain in the small of her back. Scorpion, the little kind whose sting can kill. Felt it run through her veins burning. Each lug nut a jolt through her soul.

The wind on her like spirit smashed bone. What Sun Bear had told her once during a storm, how spirit manifests itself in wind. And this one screaming holy hell, a banshee out for blood.

The green of growing things. Lifted by owl claw from the river bank where woolly mammoth once bent to drink and whose blood turned the water red during the ancestral slaughter.

Spirit wind.

And it was part of her vision, owl, green glass, tire, scorpion, pain and blood. Like giving birth, like being born, like dying and becoming wind.

She made it out, made camp on the San Juan down by the river. Bathed the wound in brown water, the wind lay down and the stars came out. How could it be that she saw them in the water, brighter even than in the sky?

Felt the offering against her thigh and said I'm sorry. Gave it to the flood plain with breath and heart and whatever a person can give beyond.

Such was her vision, Big Rose. She'd never told, not even Sun B in dreams.

7.

Yazz detested his father, which was on the difficult side, as he'd never actually met the man, and had to make him up real enough to hate. All Mama'd ever said was *don't be like him*, and then she'd shut up and never said another word about whoever *him* was again. Did he live around close. Had he killed somebody? Was he a drunk? A child molester? White? Worse? A cop? Alive? Dead? In prison? A Mormon? Partakes of the olden ways so that every last bean fart gets interpreted as spirit language? Did he like country western? Hillbilly? AC-DC? Led Zepp? Could he play guitar? Run fast? Shoot the hoop? Was he blind? An Albino? Were there even Albino Indians? A homo? Mexican? A lizard brain like Uncle Lynyrd, who wasn't even really his uncle. Left-handed or right? Blood type? Pie or cake? Could he read? Smoker? Doper? Could he get hold of weed like the Washer kid off the Rez did, long strands of black hair wound into the buds? Shiny, two feet long, blow your head off with one toke. Mouth or nose breather? Could he make it to the top of Big Mountain with a mouthful of water, like the peckerhead elders had made him do? Underwear or commando? Could he talk the olden way? Had he been burnt with fire? What exactly was he supposed to not do so as to not be like him? Say? No one would. Not even that big mouth old lady who stuck her snooty snoot into everyone's beeswax.

"You're living like you have no family," she'd said to him

once for eating the mushrooms that grew out of cow pies after a rain. She'd seen him do it from the limb-covered thing off her back porch, staring at him with those dirt colored eyes. Waiting him out at the head of the road.

The buzz was just coming on when she said it, and he was afraid he'd get laughing sickness like he always did at Indian Church when the elders got tanked on peyote buds before, during, and after.

"Maybe I don't," he'd said, and technically he was half true.

Truth was, he hated his father for not being decent enough to be a real person who he could hate, fuck with, get in a fight with on Christmas morning. The Washer kid said him and his old man always got into it on Christmas morning, just wrestling around, used to be, but real-deal fistfights since he turned sixteen and his mom said it was okay to beat the shit out of him. He'd chipped the old man's tooth, if he could tell the truth, which as far as Yazz could tell, no Washer was capable of doing.

Not with a gun to his head.

And it was contagious, wasn't it, just like Corona, which Louie'd said was named after a Mexican beer that his daddy squeezed lime in, except on Sundays when he abstained, being Catholic and all.

Why did it always have to be Sunday for Yazz. Week before Mother's Day, and mama was home watching TV, the playoffs, like Utah stood a chance in hell. Louie was supposed to pick him up, so Yazz'd thumbed a ride with the Birdman and pretty Rose Begay to the concrete court with netless goals the elders called a Recreation Center.

Now, his ball was on the flattish side, but hey, at least he wasn't munching shrooms, acting like he didn't have a family. Being like him.

Plus shooting the hoop helped him think, which he needed to do right about now, since Louie hadn't come, which could mean anything, but might mean the worst. Maybe he'd decided to test the shit out on his own. Maybe there'd been an accident, or his old man had found it and called the cops. Maybe LW was thinking to cut Yazzie out, and make a killing all by his lonesome.

It wasn't like they'd planned it all out to the tee, him and LW. But he had a car, stripped down donkey that it was, and the plates and tags were legal. Had wired a CD player up through the cigarette lighter, and hooked up to Pioneer coaxials. Could ripstomp "Back in Black," and their favorite song "Highway to Hell" though that was by the old singer, the one who OD'd. You could hear him coming before you saw him, those stoner red eyes. Spray paint horned Satan on the cinderblock wall of burned up Tsegi Trading Post.

Highway to hell! they'd scream out the open windows to the Valley of the Gods, BC[1], where they'd found the stash, the one that would make them rich enough to move to Hawaii, if LW wasn't such a donkey dick.

What he needed, Yazz, was to think. Think, think, think.

The ball ka-thunks off the goal, lays still where it lands. A gift from Uncle Lynyrd, it was a Spaulding TF-1000 microfiber composite, US Patent 45,310,178. He was instructed to "moisten the needle." To "inflate 7-9 lbs." "Indoor use only," the dark letters said, "Made in Thailand." Thailand. Where in hell is Thailand? LW claims there's good weed there, six-inch bud tied on sticks, so they call it tie-stick. Creeper deluxe, take a hit and nothing happens. Zilch. Five minutes later, whammo. Send you home to Jesus.

Mama Linda, who was a Watchtower, she used to run a scam on white people back in the old world before the Nation shut its doors. She worked for Parks and Rec over in Window Rock, and anyone wanting to backpack on Diné land had to call her up and ask for a permit. And she'd somehow gamed it so she could work from home in Dinnehotso, where the phone would ding-a-ling and she'd put on that stupid I'm an Indian dingbat voice, and tell these backpackers, and especially the river rats calling about the San Juan, the Chinle camp with Baseball Man and Star Woman, bear tracks in the drainage, she'd tell them to print out the little form titled BACKCOUNTRY PERMIT REQUEST, and say the website real slow so they could pull it up while they spoke.

"Is it up?" she'd say.

They'd get it up, these dumb-fuck river rats. What's with them, what are they smoking, anyway?

"Do you see $12 per person per day?"

Uh huh, rat said.

"How many in your party?"

Sixteen, rat said. Or sometimes twenty. And if she was real lucky and the spirits were feeling their oats, twenty-five, and they'd want a layover day at Chinle to see all the Indian shit, how sometimes washing machines washed down when the canyon flash flooded all the way from Canyon de Chelly, blew past Poncho House to the San Juan, and in October somebody—some stoned rat—would set a carved jack-o-lantern on the metal inside of the glass door, so the thing'd look like the alien in that movie.

So let's figure that. Twenty-five campers at twelve dollars a pop, throw in a third day, because why not just stop at Ledge Rapid river left and the party never ends, fuck those two black ravens who steal your weed, eat it up on the canyon face, do strategic flyovers and shit on your tent.

So, we're talking $900.00.

Mama Linda'd say, and this is the kicker, "Please mail in your money order or cashier's check to the appropriate address," which was of course their own. "All money orders or cashier's checks should be payable to Linda Watchtower, c/o Navajo Nation."

At this point, some of the rats got suspicious, coming off

their buzz. They'd say you mean I make it out to *you?* or some shit.

She wouldn't miss a beat, that dingbat Indian thing. Yazz had listened to the whole thing through enough to know, seen the checks roll in, even tried to cash them a few times and paid in skin.

"I am Parks and Recreation Representative for the Navajo Nation, and in that capacity you should make your check out to Linda Watchtower, c/o Navajo Nation. Is that clear. I will mail your permit within five business days of receipt. Will there be anything else?"

And the dumb fucks would mail their money. Mama'd send them a permit with a fake number written on it, and no one ever knew, until they did.

A riff, only a hint of sound, his first swish, and the bare bones Angus Young summoned for their third studio album, the title just right, heralds Louie Washer unseen beyond the rise. The Gibson's voice catching its breath, about to scream.

He pops again from the perimeter, Yazz, does the razzle-dazzle. Kobe's it right then left between scissored legs. Human eyes on him now, he feels connected, hardwired, only instead of LW it's that silly ass birdman, Rose Begay beside him with a smile about a foot wide.

Washer sitting beside her, that look like when he said *I shit you not* into the invisible microphone in his hand.

About to hang a u-wie.

WTF?

8.

Don't ever drive on a flat tire—you'll bend the rim, destroy the rubber and they won't be able to fix it. Of course it wasn't okay to drive over there to the first rest stop in New Mexico, Welcome to the Land of Enchantment, the sign said, Port of Entry, Entering Mountain Time Zone, Information Center, Maps and Literature. Isn't this what it's just all about? What she gets for all those breath holdings, the one-minute jolts between mile markers on what turned out to be Route 66, where she was supposed to get her kicks. And if holding your breath till you turned blue, passed out, and ran over beer bottles and shrapnel and who knows what else is how you get your kicks, well so what? And the little voice that's always inside her head, well it could just go jump in the lake, couldn't it? And if you want to drive a man crazy, just get all under his inner he-man, pull a hand crank floor jack out of the Subaru hatch, crank it so the lip fits into the weight-bearing frame groove underneath, sit cross-legged and set to jacking, forget to loosen the lug nuts, repeat.

Not yet two, she felt eyes across the asphalt, smell of rubber, heat from the lug nuts.

"You need some help?" the first one said.

"You got the E-brake on," the second.

And by the time the third man offered to do this unwomanly

deed, she'd hand tightened the nuts on the skinny-mini spare, and was jacking her down to four-way wrench it tight.

The tire's fried, lopsided rim and all. Of course it is, isn't it? Inside the air-conditioned Port of Entry, after she'd washed her hands and unmasked face, she studied the jumbo light-up map, where a red bulb marked Tucumcari as thirty miles west on 40, which was once 66, get your kicks, and a motorcycle leaned on a kickstand beneath the sign with a mannequin dressed in black leather and goggles. Best drive safe from here to the city, those tires weren't meant for much. A Sunday, she'll have to find a dealer. Subaru, the seven sisters, wasn't Luce named for stars?

Back on 40-66, anything over 60 sends the front end into a hard shimmy. She's supposed to re-tighten the lug nuts after twenty-five miles, just like she was supposed to gauge the right rear yesterday, check the oil with every fill up, don't fly with tight strings or give the D-28 to her boyfriend. And all the boatload of the rest.

The first state park is Ute Lake, named for the first sign of her birth state, Utah, *place where there are mountains*. A good sign, Ute Lake. Here in Mountain Time where she was born.

A short drive off the highway, the blue water shines against red dunes. She takes an envelope at the gate, chooses a site with a picnic table and fire pit overlooking a still cove.

Twelve dollars a night, sixteen-day limit. The whole place empty, where was everyone?

What she needed was a dog, a big black lab like Bear who they'd had to put down when she was twenty, her best friend. They'd lived on a road where sirens often wailed, and Bear'd lift snout and wolf howl, the funniest thing. What she'd thought of when the ambulance had wailed up, and they cut dad's shirt off the six fractured ribs.

Luce waded to her knees in the chill water, splashed her face and peed. The sky reflected on the water so she can't tell one from the other. What she'd do mañana, while they fix her car, find a dog, buy some food and a little water bowl that collapses so you can hike with it. Make a bed in the backseat, and not be alone forever.

There'd been a sign for a two-headed snake—a painting of it, upright and swaying like a cobra, and that's what she dreamed of in the hatch of the Subaru, the doors locked from the inside out. SEE THE TWO-HEADED SNAKE, the sign had said, the four snake eyes painted yellow with black centers. FREE ICE CREAM BEFORE THREE. IMAGINE A LAND OF MANY WONDERS. Her graduation had been virtual, beamed out from the University website to faces lit by screens from Salt Lake to Timbuktu. He'd splurged on a frame for the diploma, Dad, it was back in Florida now, with everything else. The guitar case lay beside her, the instrument handmade in the year of her birth. 1998, cusp of the millennium, a full moon in January, the Wolf, hasn't she heard the story. And he used to take her back to the hospital room she was born in, until the last time when they called security and escorted them out of the maternity, her *omphalos*, the center of her world, he said.

Waking from the dream, for just a second she doesn't know where she is, and then headlights graze the lakeside across from her and it comes back, the blow out on a Sunday just across the New Mexico line.

Wanting a dog. The two-headed snake.

Graduation.

The staged photo of her holding a fake diploma.

Visiting him in ICU.

Getting stuck in the elevator.

Wanting to get out.

Tomorrow she'll find a dealer, in Tucumcari, the name from that far away song about being willing. What did the old gunfighter say to the young? you don't have to be fast, you just have to be willing. What he said. Who knows why? Or what it meant. Could such a thing exist, a two-headed snake? The Arkansas town he'd grown up in was sometimes visited by a dead whale floated in formaldehyde in the trailer bed of a semi-truck. LEVIATHAN: MONSTER OF THE DEEP, the thing was called, he claimed. It would arrive at Knight's Grocery on Friday, payday, when Lonoke folk were cashing their checks and buying groceries, some heading to the county line for liquor. Him and his brother Jimmy'd gone once, to see Leviathan.

The late arrival sets up a tent, and a little light shines inside. They must be reading. They have a dog. She hears it bark.

She thinks of holding her breath for a highway mile. Of the barbed wire fences in Solgahatchia, blown over with honeysuckle and dust-coated blackberry bloom. Of the tombstones of unknown kin, Jimmy's, who neither she nor Mom had ever met, his smiling senior football picture from the championship team. All these other lifetimes, braided through her own. The little light goes out and she drifts in and out of sleep. What she was doing out here exactly is a guess for the ages, Ute Lake in New Mexico, not a person west of the Mississippi who'd answer a call for help. Or maybe old Nan and crazy Alex still live in Salt Lake City, Yelena and Yakov, the Kukalovs. Jack out there somewhere. There's no outrunning where you come from. She'd heard it till the cows come home, the chickens come home to roost, more times than you can shake a stick at.

Right?

Wasn't that what he said?

Florida's like living in three different countries, four if you count the Keys.

Sometimes they launch rockets from Canaveral, and if she'd got the advanced warning, she'd watch from Third Avenue Beach Access, the fine red flame bursting into an arch of sky.

Freighters couldn't use ties on their super-tall loads, because if a wind came up—if it really came a blow—they'd flip, so whatever slipped off in choppy weather was fair game. The Treasure Coast that stretch of the Atlantic was called, where Poppy'd moved when he retired from government, and Uncle Rock went to school at FIT. Mornings, the metal detectors sweep the beach, old men barefoot in the surf swing this way and that, nodding to the dog walkers and shell seekers and mystics who sit cross-legged on the sand and watch the red sun rise up out of the ocean. They'd been going there forever, she knows all the landmarks and restaurants and where Meemaw's ashes are in the grassy lot in front of St. Sebastian-by-the-Sea. Spanish galleons had sunk off the coast, and Ponce de León was supposed to have landed just down the beach in search of the Fountain of Youth. Nights were spectacular. All light was banned because of the turtles who'd only swim into the dark dunes to lay eggs, and if you got lucky you'd see one's luminescent body in the breakers, and watch it make the long crawl up to a dune and go to digging. Once she found two coins in different places, both from 1974, and that night she'd seen a turtle, so that something must have happened in that year to make it lucky for her. She'd have to look it up, 1974. A long time ago. Ancient history.

Inside the tent on the other side of the lake, the little light had gone out, so turtles might crawl there, except for the dog. The sound of guitar comes to her clean and faint, all wrapped in the gauzy fabric of dream.

9.

Before she dropped out and married and became the sort of person she'd become, Joanna had applied and been accepted to a study abroad in Tours, France, about as far away from Vernal as she was ever likely to get. There was a cathedral there, in Tours, at the heart of the city. Beautiful and old and jam-packed with the sort of art that's painted for people who can't read. Joanna'd proposed to study the portrayal of women in religious imagery, and wasn't that just right up her alley? The professor who wrote her letter of recommendation said:

> ...Having grown up in Vernal, Utah, a town on the edge of Wyoming and Colorado, Ms. McCreary possesses frontier verve and common sense, yet seems perfectly at home in the fast-paced curriculum of the University Honors College. As a person, she is humorous, kind, and bold. She has certainly experienced firsthand the treatment of women in patriarchal systems, and is therefore uniquely situated for her proposed project. I believe that you will find her a wonderful student abroad, and a genuine asset in all situations. I recommend her highly and without hesitation.
>
> Sincerely,
> Joseph Harvell, Ph.D.
> Distinguished Honors Professor
> University of Utah

Put that in your pipe and smoke it. Hang your hat on it. *Frontier verve* and *common sense*. It was a French noun, *verve*. *Fantasy, caprice, animation. Special ability or talent. Spirit. Enthusiasm. Energy. Vitality.*

She keeps the letter and the picture postcard of the cathedral in a place where no one could ever find it, but of course *he* did, just like he found out everything else. And once somebody knows something like that about you, that you'd actually believed in those words and held their truth to your heart, well they've got you cooked, don't they? A genuine *asset* in all situations, how he'd say the word, just a genuine *asset* in all situations. He could go straight to heck, Roger could. How different her life might have been if she'd gone, broke bread in the bistros of that little French town, sipped cabernet on afternoons while pouring over the colorful women of the Bible—the three Marys, Bathsheba, the Woman Taken in Adultery. St. Apollonia, whose tormenters pulled out her teeth, dressed like a rainbow. The Magdelenes with their nightlights and ascending doves. St. Sebastian tended by Irene. Rebecca at the well. In her own good time and verve, Judith Beheading Holofernes, how she'd got him drunk and used his own sword. Go girl.

Back home, she might have taken a job in Special Collections, crated online lectures for the poor, suffering students staring at screens during the black plague. Could have, should have, would have. But here she was in Vernal, and it's May already. Another year, this one as a masked teller at First Credit, making deposits for men newly rich from the gas and oilfields over in Dinosaur.

A genuine *asset*, Joanna.

Her father the Bishop preaching this morning, and if she was there in the Temple which was not one thing on earth like the Tours Cathedral, he'd stare straight at her the whole time, speak of vice and the failure of faith and service to the bridegroom, how a reckoning was at hand for the wicked, surely it was. Mom didn't buy it, but what could she do? He knew her celestial name, would call her across space and time and she'd have to come. What'd Roger'd said that last night, *I'll call your name and you'll come.*

The creek behind her apartment's at flood stage. She hears it out there, going at it. Makes her have to pee. She hears it at night, gets into her dreams, the river.

How they'd met, on the river. A hundred years ago, a thousand. Eight to be precise. August, 2013. Her Honors College cohort had done a river trip on Lodore Canyon through Parks & Rec. It was supposed to help them bond, being on the river, suffering some together, cooking, using a communal groover. Sixteen of them from Humanities, they'd strapped on PFDs and stuffed dry bags with ten times too many clothes, sunscreen, guitars and river journals, sunglasses and tampons, weed, rigged at the Gates over at Maybell. August, the water was low. *Bony*, the cute oarsman guide said when they put on, and drifted through the Gates of Lodore which had a famous poem written about it that he could quote. He'd break into it when you least expected, the cute guide.

Her and giggling Angelina Gills, who they joked could breathe underwater, bow babes in front of the gear boat, the stern loaded down with a stove and propane, hand wash stations and dry bags, whiskey back there, though it wasn't allowed, nosiree.

"Through meadow and glade, in sun and in shade," he'd say, those big oarsman hands wrapped around handles of the ten foot shafts, and they lay back and take the sun, cold splash sometimes, they suffered and bonded.

The rapids were always named for something awful. Upper and Lower Disaster, the second of which had an undercut cave with a red kayak stuck deep in its shadow on river right. A channel above a tiny rock island pouring that way.

"What's that," she'd asked.

"Rising and leaping, sinking and creeping, a place to stay out of," he said.

For some reason, the red kayak stuck in shadow stayed with her, fit with what came after, and after that. How on the third day they'd floated around a bend at a placed called Island Park in Echo Canyon, the confluence with the Yampa where their party was supposed to fill up with water and visit a cave with petroglyphs and sweet cold air like being in an icehouse in the dead of summer. Only when they turned the bend at Steamboat Rock, the whole island was covered with cops who were clearly waiting on them to arrive, hands shielding sun from their eyes, scoping them through binoculars, some of them, in uniforms, wearing guns.

"And dashing and flashing and splashing and clashing," the boat captain said, as the cops motioned them in.

And the one who'd met their boat, took the line and tied it to the trunk of a Russian Olive. You know who. "You'll have to stay here a while," he said. "There's a party behind you."

"And so never ending, but always descending."

"Excuse me?"

"It's a poem he's been saying for us."

Roger didn't smile, not in the least. "There's been a fatality," he said. And that was it. The first time Joanna met Roger Doyle Stoner, who'd remember her at the takeout two days later, when the afternoon sun had taken some of the chill off that had come over the whole party, watching the parents arrive at Echo Park to unload their sad cargo.

He'd remember her, and her last name put him in mind of his Ward's Bishop in Vernal, and what a surprise, her father. Would she like to go to the Dino Rodeo with him next weekend? He'd pick her up in a squad car, and she could talk on the radio. Would that be okay?

The end of the river trip with the red kayak stuck in her head. What else was she going to do?

The reasons to get the heck out of Vernal the first chance you get are myriad. A small

Utah, backwood Mormon town, it's got big with the mining west of town, gas and oil and fracking everything that's frackable, the potash and phosphate mine dug into forty square miles on the hills to the north, upon which sits an asphalt pad with a shaded scenic overlook built for viewers to gaze out on the split stone mountain where river and wind have worn the earth to bare bone and whole dinosaur skeletons and skulls and obscene leg bones big as cars are found by the trainload in what is known as the richest fossil field on earth. What anybody with three dollars can see at Dinosaur Quarry Museum built right over the dig, an exposed wall of bone and skull and vertebrae that will take your head off, or it should, because it was right there in your face proof that the Book of Mormon and the Bible and just about everything people believed in and prayed to was a big load of *ca-ca*. No, Earth was not four thousand years old, and when men died they did not get their own planet, and her secret name was just a goddamn word some knuckle-head had made up, instead of a summons from eternity.

She'd bought a postcard there at the Quarry Museum. On it was a partially excavated skull and neck vertebrae, teeth embedded in the jaw, an eye hole, tiny face bones that had, heretofore, never been seen before. *Skull of Camarasaurus*, it says on back, *from a long-necked plant eater.*

She mailed it to herself, Joanna. Just so she wouldn't forget. It's in the holy book this second, damning it to hell, if there is a hell other than the Hadean Eon 4,500 million years ago, when there was no evidence for life on Earth, and whose name translates to hellish.

Leave it to the town fathers, of which her father was certainly chief among, to turn the truth of the dinosaurs into high farce, create Dino Days, with a Miss Dino waving from the saddle on the back of smiling Dopey the Dinosaur, painted froggy green and configured so its tail wagged side to side, followed by Dopey's pink-painted sister, and what Joanna's always thought of as the pair's cross-eyed inbred offspring, Dopey Junior, on display at the Dino Museum just off Main street, where no one was stirring this morning, because it was Sunday and you'd be scorned, and no one could scorn like Vernal scorners, could they?

One good thing, Colorado's only twenty-five miles away. A whole other state where you could buy beer on Sunday, which is what Joanna's of a mind to do, because it just tastes better in Colorado on a Sunday by the river which made wordless music so as to outsing the saints to kingdom come.

She gassed the truck Daddy'd given her, his plates on it. Hopped on I-40 and headed east.

Tossing and crossing, flowing and going.

10.

Crazy little bastards'll blow their asses to smithereens, won't they, though what exactly was a *smithereen?* Rose's dictionary, a duct-taped *Webster New Collegiate* that stays on the kitchen table says "bits." *The house was blown to smithereens by the explosion*, says the example. Above smithereens is *smite*. What God did to Indians by turning them from beauteous white to heinous red—*He did so smite them for their sin*. That's the problem with dictionaries, all those words. Could you even say that in Navajo, *He did so smite them for their sin?* They don't have a Navajo dictionary, is there even such a thing? Rose'd know, first Sunday in May, off somewhere in the Monument with that birdy-bird man.

Nephew done snuck into the birdhouse, taken an egg or three, each with *unknown* written on it as if to answer the question of why they were buried in BC[1] to begin with, where they came from and why. In Apache School down in Chiricahua, teacher'd taught Lynyrd the five elements holy to any story worth its salt: who, what, where, when, why, how. And the thing about going to Apache school in Chiricahua is that they won't teach you how to say "salt" in Apache because the language is dangerous, you might catch the building on fire or some shit. And salt was of course holy, so you probably weren't even supposed to go around saying it, were you?

At the kitchen table, with its foil covered window that

would otherwise be looking north toward the Blue Abajo and Bear's Ears, Lynyrd, whose best friend at Apache school was a shaved-headed trouble maker named Kennard, prints the word—s a l t with a pencil that needs sharpening, only the pencil sharpener is in Big Rose's room, and that's off limits to anyone and everyone, believe you me. Find the word for it. Because words were power. You could own something by knowing its name.

Take Yazz, for example. Yazzie Watchtower. Navajo. Diné. Yazzie was both a given and a surname, and it was not uncommon to come across a Yazzie Yazzie, so there was good medicine in the word, it had some snap, crackle and pop about it. Good vowels—the *a* and the *e* with the *zs* buzzing in between. You could chop it off and add to *ie*, either way. And don't even get started with the Watchtower part. Before you knew it you'd be knee-deep in Kit Carson and Canyon de Chelly, the siege on Navajo Mountain and the long march there and back again. Give Big Rosey a child's portion of jug wine and she'd just go on and on. So what he's thinking, Lynyrd, is that you could know a whole lot about a person by looking at their name.

He knew a boy back home whose daddy'd named him Lucky, and the kid had ended up at a facility for fuck ups, which just so happened to be housing Merle Haggard at the time, who'd throw a little concert every afternoon for residents, sing "Mama Tried" and "If We Make it Through December" three times apiece if you asked.

He'd once known a Cleopatra who wrote poetry.

Jefferson Davis.

Three or four Geronimos and a Cochise.

Sometimes people changed their names to something that fit better. Like the boy in that Johnny Cash song whose daddy'd named him Sue. Or, say, if the Apache mother who'd one day kick you out of the family because sons weren't allowed to stay, say she'd named you Roy, which rhymed with boy, why you'd go out and find something better, take one from that long-haired hippy band you liked who'd named themselves after their high school principal down in Florida.

Lynyrd was a good name, he liked it fine.

It was salt.

But *Unknown?*

Big Rose said Bird Man, whose real name was Edgar, if he told the truth, knew the answer. Would that be *who*, or *what?* Could a thing be both at the same time like he was Lynyrd and Roy, and salt was a rock and money that traded pound for pound with gold once upon a time?

Back when he'd first got here, nobody'd touch that cave with a ten-foot pole, and now this. More where that comes from, nephew claims. But what on earth did you do with it, dynamite with handwriting on it. He was in agreement, Lynyrd, that they should test it out first, see if they were duds or the real McCoy.

"When?" Nephew'd asked.

"Where?" Uncle'd countered, who, what and how being covered already.

Outside, a truck thunka-thunks, Thelma barks once, then Louise. Big Rosey's bed squeaks, and the sound of a basketball being dribbled in the dirt, the jolt of it off the side of the house. Not yet hot, as fine a day as any, they'll ride the Sunday out on the limb-covered back porch and listen to the creek, the white horse neigh, and today, hear the jingle-jangle story of how dynamite, TNT, blow your butt to the big house, came to be buried in Big Cave One, and what to do since it had been discovered there by the two young hoodlums who'd just arrived in the bed of Bird Man's Chevrolet, a strange name for a truck, was it French?

Big Rosey says to brew coffee.

"I did, already," Lynyrd said.

"More."

She wafts smoke from a juniper branch through the kitchen, out the sliding glass door to the back porch, turns Rez Radio on, The Circle of Life, southern drum, pow wow stuff. She means business, Big Rose. Everything happens for a reason, she says. Everything. Even this.

He wishes Rita was here to take the edge off, but she's at the bridge, big Kuya against her knee under the table, selling mojos. They'd have to pray. Lynyrd's sure they'll have to pray and the drums on the radio will boom-boom, and Big Rose'll say something unintelligible in Navajo, and everyone will nod and pretend they know what's what.

He grinds more coffee beans in the little grinder, packs five good-smelling spoonsful into the Mr. Coffee filter, dumps in a potful of water from a gallon jug filled with the good stuff from the gas station.

She's starting frybread, Big Rose, usually his job, he can make it in his sleep. The flour and lard, good salt. The smell will hang under the arbor and mix with their talk.

And he does have some splainen to do, doesn't he, Bird. Who, what, where, when, why and how. And now Mama Linda's got word of the whole mess, good god what she'll come up with—get them all up shit creek. Not like the black plague and the curfews and shut down nation so nobody floats the rivers and there goes his swamping money, but at least the man's stayed away, afraid to breathe the same air as Indians. Now there's a vaccination drive, with the goal of putting a needle into every red arm in Four Corners, a drive through over in Bluff at Recapture Lodge. There's word of reopening for the Solstice in June, the river and monument tours. Went through their house like a brush fire, poor skinny bird caught the chill. Wasn't like he was worthless. He had fixed their electric and dug the well house out, so it worked for a while, though the water was laced with whatever peach face pumped into the river upstream. He didn't trust it unless it came out of a jug.

But they had water, for a while they had. The dogs drank it and didn't die.

Speak of the devil.

Bird Man and Little Rose, Yazzie with a bball going hand to hand. They come under the arbor from the back way, ducking to miss the lowest limbs. Woolly-headed Washer boy in tow. There'll be six of them, best carry out kitchen chairs, an ashtray, paper plates.

On the table, Roses dictionary's still opened to *smithereens.* Just below *smite—he did so smite them for their sin.*

11.

The source of the music, the light, the tent, and the dog, is gone by daylight, and the Subaru smells just like somebody slept in it and of course there's no dealership in Tucumcari, nor any of the podunk towns before Albuquerque, which is too many miles to drive on the skinny spare, but just what else is she supposed to do? Mom's given her the full report of her road status, offered to pull AAA in from Melbourne Beach, three quarters of a continent away. Boy oh boy. She could have it towed, but don't you need a back tire for that? What she could use was breakfast, mile high biscuits and gravy like she used to eat at the lodge before floating the Green River about a hundred years ago. Before COVID and the whole boatload that came with it. "I can't do much for you from here," Mom had said. And it was true. The whole thing had been a sore spot between them, but, hey, she'd turn twenty-five this year, and what was Mom doing at that age besides traipsing across Europe on a Eurorail pass, keeping the journal that daddy once referred to as *Emmanuelle Goes to Europe*. "That's not fair," she said. Right it wasn't.

"You shouldn't have driven on the rim."

She shouldn't have driven on the rim.

"Are you going to be okay?"

She'd be okay.

"How far is Albuquerque?"

Two hundred miles, something like that.

"The dealership's named Fiesta."

She said, *"Buen Camino."*

"Are you talking and driving?"

She was talking and driving.

"Is it pretty there?"

Drop dead.

"Call when you get there."

She'd call when she got there.

Her hair was still wet. Before leaving Ute Lake, she'd bathed in the chill water, washed with Doc Bronner's peppermint, dried off and dressed in clean shorts and a t-shirt. Not a cloud in the sky, and the light really was different, somehow more golden, and not at all the red fireball that rose up out of the Atlantic. She thought she'd heard the dog splashing before she got up, running after a stick, playing fetch. She purposefully turns off NPR—let the news of the world be. She drove slow, semis blowing by. She willed herself there, to Fiesta where they'd charge her an arm and a leg. What he'd say, an arm and a leg. What that guitar'd cost, no doubt. You could trade it for a car. What was this Edgar Paris so important for, to just give it away. She can smell it back there, the wood has an aroma. Rosewood from India, Mahogany, Sitka Spruce. The rules: don't give it to your boyfriend, keep humidified, loosen strings before flight.

She'd met him, Paris. He'd stayed with them way back when, spoke with the same accent as Dad, only more. Lived in the basement with the Bear-ghost, her best friend dog they'd had to put down.

Albuquerque or Bust, a hitchhiker's cardboard sign says. She rolls on with the windows down—a three-hour drive at sixty, a mile a minute, a single breath held from signpost to signpost, the miles getting smaller one to the next.

How long did it take to get out of Limbo?

What came after?

Her story. There'd been Jack, non-Mormon Jack. Growing up in Salt Lake, you just wouldn't believe. She's past all that.

Way past.

At the Flying J outside Clines Corners, she fills up, uses the window washer squeegee on the windshield, locks it before going to pee. Buys an apple pie wedge at the checkout. Outside is parked the truck source of last night's music, she's sure of it. They were going the same way, north to Four Corners and west to Dinnehotso. And where then. She's looking for the sign. Pray for it, Dad'd say. In a good way. Not like the derelict Utah governor who'd instructed citizens to pray for rain because of the climate change from hell drought.

She had a degree. Human Development and Family Studies. Had done the year with AmeriCorps, and then the trip to Guatemala and Argentina. Back in the old world with people who carried current U.S. passports and you could still leave the country.

A dog's snout pokes through the window crack, breathes.

"You're a good dog, aren't you."

Back on the road, she can feel every bump through the skinny spare. Help me get there, she says. Close to a prayer, if not.

In Albuquerque, she follows Mom's text, finds Fiesta Subaru, hands over her key. Luce waits in a customer center with popped corn and ice cream machines, a soda fountain and latte brewer—is latte a brew? A giant TV with a woman baking biscuits on it, magazines and tire displays, roof racks and a platform that sits on top of your car so you can set up a tent and sleep on the roof, for whatever reason anyone would want to do that. Snakes, raccoons, like the wandering monsters that had broke into the chicken coop that September before daddy's fall. He'd forgot to lock the gate. Well, they all had, it was sort of a group job. But they'd forgot, that's what matters.

A party was going on across the street at the ski house, so none of them could hear the chickens screaming bloody murder, the raccoons—surely there was more than one for that kind of carnage—chewing the heads off one before going to the next. They'd killed the Speckled Sussex from the first flock, the one she'd named Spots as a girl, and had grown up with. He'd had to put her out of misery with a shovel. How she'd watched him out there pounding its head with the broad side, and they'd buried it, wrapped in blue sage and red yarn, said prayers. One had lived. The biggest Black Sex Link, it's comb chewed full off and one eye chewed out. She'd nursed it and it lived, even laid again. He'd called it Cyclops, and its survival lifted his heart, so he said, after the fall.

She'd never seen a live raccoon, Luce.

But such would drive her to sleep on the roof, though weren't they good climbers? Didn't dog hunters shoot them from trees? Wasn't there a saying, run you up a tree?

The popped corn is salty, and the woman on the giant TV grates butter into her biscuit dough.

She needs water.

The nice service rep smiles like its Christmas, tells her that she has a leaky head gasket, and had she had her timing belt replaced at 125 K? They should have replaced the water pump with the belt, did she remember? Have paperwork? She was a quart and a half low, they'd refill on the house. All the other fluids. Drop in a new air filter. And, oh yeah. There was this thing about computer systems in Subarus that meant all four tires had to have the same tread depth, otherwise the all-wheel drive malfunctioned, and you were right back where you started from. What this meant, he mansplained to her, was that she had two options: the first, which was his preferred solution, was to purchase four steel-belted Yokohamas, along with the new rim, have them all mounted and balanced, and they'd throw in an alignment. She could opt for roadside service, just in case. That was the way to go, the safest bet. Option two was to buy a new tire and have it shaved down to the tread height of the other three, counting on them all having worn the same, which was usually not the case, with missed rotations and so on, life was life. The new tires were in stock, and the rim which they could discount with the tire package. Otherwise, the shaver was out of shop, and she'd have to leave the car overnight for service. Would she prefer Option 1? Or shaving a new tire?

He was so nice, the service rep, letting her know the options. He could keep her around a thousand, fifteen hundred, tops. But that head gasket wasn't going anywhere, was it?

They'd get right on it. Just say the word.

12.

191 ran north to Flaming Gorge Dam and Dutch John and the stretch of Green where you could hook Browns the length of your calf on gold Rapalas, fifty in a day when it was hot. And it was true enough that the next town over was Vernal, where there was a certain POI for Officer Roger Stoner, though that was secondary, wasn't it. First things first. He had business with the Arky. Last seen at the state line, about to cross over. Arkansas DMF 936, brake light out, passenger side. Half-ton Jimmy, blue with white trim. Same vehicle he'd driven before arrest, multiple offenses, resisting, exposure, vandalism, defamation, urinating in public. Assault on an Officer of the Peace. Blasphemy. Sixty days in, sixty out. With professor peckerhead. The Harvell boy. Who, of all the fat chance synchronicities ever to come his way, had been the very history prof who'd written the double dog bullshit letter recommending Joanna for a study abroad, the one she'd backed out of before they were married—in the Temple, by big brother. She'd kept it hidden, the letter. Like he couldn't find it. A trophy to the snot-nose coed she'd been before they met.

He turns north at Kayenta, Monument Valley all lit up between him and Utah, and the three-day cold trail of Edgar Paris, living with Indians, the Begay girl, Rose, she should know better. Taking up with a man like that.

He could use coffee, Stoner. Why'd he have to go and think of Joanna, always dogging him, day in day out.

Out here, distance is deceptive.

His Bishop Daddy'd thrown him under the bus summer before ninth grade. Sent him off with a *wilderness therapy* program because he'd got in trouble that once, and graduating from the program would keep it off his record, and make him a better person, to boot. His father had actually paid money for the therapy, which amounted to getting hauled off to south Utah and left alone in the desert for four days and nights without food and water, nor blanket. Nothing at all but a piece of string, with which he was to make fire, and thus roast pinyon nuts to keep from starving. Pick them off the ground. Lick morning dew off chokecherry leaves. Seek a vision. A reason to be. It had been out there somewhere that far-off objects started to play tricks with him. Bears Ears, the Seven Sailors over to Valley of the Gods, the Lukachukai and San Francisco peaks—how they vacillated on the plot of earth that was his symbolic grave, where he was to leave his old self to make way for the new, improved version. The long mountain named Sleeping Ute, with an aspen grove growing over the heart of what looked, from a distance, like a horizontal body. And the trees were all one organism, with leaf like fire when the sun got at them right. Close and far off at the same time.

"Don't look at me. You're dead," the Indian had said.

And it had got dark, and he forgot about the string and pinyon nuts, but the thought of water made him crazy, and it took forever for the night to pass for dew to fall on the chokecherry leaves, each the shape of a tongue.

The stars and planets bouncing like beach balls and it was as cold then as it was hot in the day, so the senses sharpened and you could smell stones and hear Sleeping Ute's tree heartbeat and taste the hour to hour passage of time yaw-yawing in all directions.

His anger passed. And there was a quiet place. So maybe he *had* become a better person out there in the desert summer before ninth grade. Maybe he had. But what good was that now, his desire for chase perfectly balanced with his need to make right with his wife, who he loved and was sealed to for eternity.

Say?

Sleeping Ute, you listening? You still out there, tree man?

And what kind of person gives you a piece of string and tells you to make fire? It was possible, though unlikely. They'd showed him how. One of the therapists, this girl somebody must have done pretty bad, because was she ever some kind of pissed, teaching teen delinquents to make bow and spindle, a nest of juniper bark. Loop the spindle, set it to the nest which lay on a stone cleft, draw the bow, once, twice before smoke, then a punk of bright coal, blow breath into flame. He'd seen it happen, alright. Best magic trick ever. And he'd mastered it in time. Making fire. And wasn't that what separated us from animals?

Fire.

He'd been in a hole too long. What was he going to do with Paris once he caught him? And for just a second, driving down a road that is straight as it is long, the balance shifted. For one perceivable second, it did.

He'd tell her her secret name. His. If that's what it took, he would. She could call him and he'd come. Stoner would.

The hell with big brother and the rules. Threats. All of that. It was a load, wasn't it. All about keeping you afraid. And what did fear have to do with it, the truth?

Only a supreme act of will keeps him from hanging a U-wie that second and heading north. They'd had a garden in Page, that first year. She'd planted snow peas that had burned up before they'd got three pickings, but so what? Joanna walked him out back first thing of an April morning, snapped a handful from amongst white blooms and neon green, and they were sweet and good when he tasted them. She'd smiled and nodded and touched his face with her hand, so he'd breathed in the aroma that was her and the vine, and is there anything on this earth hopeful as planting peas in the desert?

Another day, he'll cross the state line into Utah, *Life Elevated* the sign says. Officially within his jurisdiction, Stoner kills the radio, goes commando with windows rolled down, good air cut with sage and maybell. He'd once tried to live in a city, Greensboro, North Carolina, to be exact, where they'd sent him and Dusty Jensen to save gentile souls. Daddy'd pulled a string to get him the gig. And he'd tried. Had he ever. He'd read the word, memorized the spiel, had the suit and the hair-cut and smile down pat, how to be patient and let the target think they were leading the conversation. Shared interest, find common ground. Dusty was from Duschesne, just off the Ute Rez, so North Carolina might as well have been the moon for them both, the unspeakable heat morning, noon and night. Sleet in winter. The way the people gargled vowels like mouth-fuls of marbles. How they worshipped at the altar of barbecue and basketball, everybody and their mother a smoker. Hell, they grew the shit there, tobacco barns all across Guilford and Alamance Counties, fields of it growing out of red dirt. Place called the Piedmont, which meant at the foot of mountains, and if those were mountains he'd kiss the ass of every Tarheel from Morehead City to Asheville.

He'd got used to them hating him. Serving them hash-laced brownies and sweet tea, let's go sit in the shade of the backyard, sonny boys, and can I bring my guitar? When I talk about Jesus I like to have my guitar.

The women smiling, looking at the floor. Some with crushes on them because there were men of god, in suits, blessed with magical powers, maybe, to consecrate ground and make a space holy—they didn't know it, maybe, but suspected.

He'd been passed more than one phone number. Ditto Dusty.

They'd been instructed on the strategies of dealing with impure thoughts, especially at night when the window unit air conditioners moaned and it came on hard, and a young missionary was pulled toward fleshly desire for all that was carnal in that southland of the heart.

Number One: when the impure thought comes, try thinking of that moment in the cloud room when they sat on the goat's back and so passed to the beast all sin, past, present and future. How they'd tasted the butchered animal that very eve, shared meat and drink with who they loved. His goat had bleated and curled up its lips so the image of the lips and slitty eyes, and that ungodly voice bleating up through the clouds. Uh huh, forget about it. Number Two: Chinese Medicine. When the big nasty came on, the young priest was supposed to remove one of the jumbo binder clips from their Instructionary Paper Work for Outward Bound Missionaries and clip it to the offending appendage. That's what the Elders called it, *offending appendage.*

"For how long," young Stoner'd asked.

His teacher had smiled, tranquilly, as if remembering his own episodes with the beasts of southern wilds. "It varies," he'd said. "from one to another."

About three seconds.

That's how long it took Stoner to bypass Number Two. Even if it worked, you had to get up in the dark and find your paperwork, and by then, why bother?

Number Three: Make a sandwich. That's right. Go to the fridge, get out the meat and cheese, mustard and mayo. Ketchup if you liked. Pickles. Toast your bread, or don't. Make the sandwich. Eat. Go back to bed.

Don't call the numbers unless they're serious about salvation, and you have the obligation to follow up.

He'd been sent home short of the first year, black sheep, black sheep, black sheep. And now he was a cop, a trooper, on the tail of a fugitive who'd maybe violated probation three years ago, in the Old World before the plague and suffering. When Joanna's voice had inflicted invective on him recently enough to be recalled—the space between the words, how they shook the light fixture, no getting away from it.

What had hurt him worst about living east was simple claustrophobia. When you've stood on your front porch and seen a hundred miles, like he can this very second, from Mexican Hat to Valley of the Gods. How are you supposed to live and breathe where you can't see across the street?

A little blonde-headed girl had met them at the screen door on Stoner's last day. "Which one of you wants to be kicked in the balls first?" she'd asked, and that was that.

Stoner was on his way home next day, somebody else on the way to make sandwiches with Dusty. So, if you counted up through the present, Stoner'd managed to fail at every substantial endeavor he'd ever attempted.

He'd have to face his failures.

Man up.

Isn't that what they said?

13.

Big Rose fanned smudge this way and that, around the circle where they sat under her limb-covered back porch, protected just a little from the heat that was coming, though it was only May, first Sunday. How Edgar'd got there from Illinois Bayou where he'd first gone under that Sunday in another age, when preacher'd held him down till he came up fighting for breath, reborn, met by the voices of his kith and kin, saints gathered there at the river, the beautiful, beautiful river, is a question for the ages. And now here he was with Indians, a whole powwow circle of them save the Washer kid, Edgar Paris, come to Parley what to do with the hundred and forty sticks of high grade dynamite he'd retrieved from Navajo Bridge, because you couldn't just leave it there, could you, each one writ with the name of a member of the Fancher Party who'd been massacred at Mountain Meadows in New Harmony at the hand of John D. Lee, who carried out the command of the high prophet, kill every one of them old enough to tell the tale, and that's what they'd bygod done, hadn't they, September 11, 1849, dressed as Indians, so help him God.

Rose has Lynyrd beat on the drum some, commences to pray. At first in that hard talky-talk to hook up to Great Spirit, then in regular old language that made sense. She sat smoking in a silver lawn chair with some of the mesh straps broken through, her eyes shut, making prayer with smoke and sound.

He got nervous when Indians prayed, Edgar. They'd go onto Indian time and before you knew it tomorrow'd come and they were still talking, eyes shut, some of them crying out a little when they felt like the speaker'd hit a good part. There was Lynyrd, Big and Little Rose, Yazz and the Washer kid and Edgar, and from around the corner walked Mama Linda Watchtower to make it seven, the only one missing, Rita, up at the bridge with a .357 magnum between her knees, point up at unsuspecting tourists come to buy Indian mojos, and Stoner earlier this morning, he was on the way. So, reason to make haste. Pray.

For rain and the river and creepy crawlies, two and four-legged, the flying ones and the still. That we might all leave what doesn't serve us in this place right now and move forward in a good way. For our ancestors that they might know we hold them to our hearts and consider seven generations into the future with every decision, so that our descendants will know our hearts, our minds and spirits and bodies. For those who come and those who go, judges and surgeons and medicine workers so under travail now with the black death aloose from here to Timbuktu. For the young whose restless spirits were uprooted and blowing on a wind of rebelliousness and meanness and downright get in your face highway to hell disregard for what was good and decent, who lived as if they had no families.

Little squeals went out from Mama Linda and Rose. Lynyrd said *aho*, and the Washer boy nodded. Yazz was oblivious, none of this meant a thing to him, an unbeliever, which was necessary for a prayer circle, Edgar'd learned, along with a holy clown and a *wain-tay*, sometimes one in the same, someone to beat on a drum and another to say the words. So the day undoes itself and becomes prayer, sometimes it does.

She asks blessings for the seven directions: up, down, on either side, front and back, inside. For father sun and earth mother, and the blue-blue window behind the stars. For the still place that rests inside spirals glyphed in desert varnished stone on Bears Ears, and the living tree-heart of Sleeping Ute, even though he was ancient enemy to the Diné, time had come to lay down the implements of hurting, to set Kuya aside and seek new balance, attune themselves to the drumbeat of true hearts. Thank you for giving them this to do, great mystery, have pity, they were weak and trusted wrongly, made prayers with no associated actions. For lost white brother and communion to come, for the medicine man and the vaccine he'd brought to the Nation. For their houses and land, tree and nut. For the good earth they walked on and the privilege of doing so. For family. Drum. Water. Sky.

For songs and the twisting flute of each voice singing.

For the vision that was and the one that will be. Bear, wolf, eagle, antelope. Hawk. Fish. Raven. The willow people. Creepy crawlers and Iktome. The great horned owl who'd flown up on speckled wings the day she had her vision at the Butt Formation over in Butler Wash, when she'd walked to the cedar and the land unfolded itself to her and she could see—the painted kiva and water works, the birthing stone and place of naming, the lookout where pottery was made, a stone for skinning, metate for grinding. When the afternoon sun went golden and she found her way, and then she didn't. A piece of green glass, worn smooth, lay on the altar, she sees it again, Big Rose, green of growing things, all that matters in this world. How some medicine comes to you twice and you know it for the first time.

By now even Yazzie was thrumming with it, the smokey cadence sing-songing under shade boughs. Blue sage, azilia, copal, tobacco and the smell of rain.

There at the altar of time and space. Where holy ones shed their skin and walked to the mountain, Sleeping Ute, the white boughs of Aspen, green bottle glass, worn smooth, grasped by talon then beak, a gift from Corn Maiden to the people, dusted with yellow pollen, snake danced and cherished, all that was alive and living. The green of growing things, mother of life, mother of death.

She prayed that way, Big Rose. Edgar said *aho*, meant it. The mothership of words at last airborne.

And her great blind spot is healed. She leaves it be. Forgive her, father, she did not know what she'd done. Green of growing things, of tomorrow and what came before, wind on water, air before a tornado, scorpion sting, banshee out for blood. A jolt through her soul.

The wind on them like spirit smashed bone. What Sun Bear had told her once during a storm, how spirit manifests itself in wind. And this one screaming holy hell, out for blood.

The green of growing things. Lifted by owl claw from the river bank where woolly mammoth once bent to drink and whose blood turned the water red during the ancestral slaughter.

Spirit wind.

She had Yazz now, he was cooked.

And it was part of her vision, owl, green glass, tire, scorpion, pain and blood. Like giving birth, like being born, like dying and becoming wind.

Such was her vision, Big Rose. On this day in the Valley of the Gods. Sun B listening. The girl with her babe draped in the face scalp. The ones from before. After.

And what could it teach them now?

Say?

They had conceived to write the names of the murdered dead on sticks of dynamite, that was already done. And then they'd wired it to a bridge that the elders had termed Koyanisqatsi, world out of balance. Intended to blow it up, then didn't. Angels had descended at the last second, a life was spared, the very one headed toward them this second. The Harvell boy'd found a hair pin at the meadows, blonde hair woven through the clasp. One of the girls', it was the green of growing things, and he'd chosen not to blow the bridge, to take life, had given it to the river, the green clasp.

Then Edgar'd chiseled out the lot of it, and at her bidding buried it in BC[1] where they'd once dug up a two-thousand-year-old teenage girl with her baby, and she'd been wearing a green-painted scalp, just like the green face painted on the cliff face at Sand Island, where she'd bathed the scorpion sting all those years ago. And now the young folks had abandoned belief and dug up some of it there. Not all, just a bundle. A medicine bundle with them that second. Wired together, a bouquet.

How to see the mystery through, past their great blind spot. Translate for them, have pity. For the weak who lack trust. Help.

Drumbeat, and then the sending home the spirits song, the sudden smell of frybread through the screen door. Evening coming on, shades on far off plateaus to the Utah line and beyond.

Help, they'd prayed.

Translate the mystery.

Please.

Have pity.

And thank you. Most of all, thank you.

They listen, lift eyes for the sign, because it's coming, surely it is. No accidents in this life. *Metakuye Oyasin.*

Green of growing things, truth come rolling.

14.

That day she drove into Arizona, Window Rock, tribal capitol for the Navajo Nation, with her new head gasket and timing belt, riding on unshaved tires, Luce Harvell was received by the birthplace of her father, and the day was bright and good. The land had a look about it, wide open with a red backbone that shone as a moonscape, the view from on high of the delta riverbeds, land of the Hopi and Paiute, Navajo, and not so far from where Geronimo had begged freedom to return so that he might die near the plum tree where his mother'd buried his birth sack. It fills the eye, this place, here and now. Like a toothache, Daddy'd say, in a hot house on an August night when rabbits squeal in Arkansas.

Mom's beach towel is over the Martin, draped so her name shines in the rearview where New Mexico gives way and Luce drives head on into the land of the woolly-headed Washers. 191 through Chinle, which must be the same Chinle as the wash they sometimes camped on the San Juan, just above Mule Ear, fossilized throat of an extinct volcano that had spewed garnets for a mile in all directions. On a layover day, she'd filled two inches of a sandwich baggie with rust-red birthstones from ant-hills. What happened to them, her garnets?

Like holding the flannel shirt of someone you loved and would never see again to your face, breathing them in, that kind of here and now that is neither and both at the same time. Six days out from Florida, or seven? Summer in front of her, on the heels of the plague. Fifty-six miles from Dinnehotso, a sign says, with First, Second, and Third Mesas west. The only radio station is in another language, Navajo? Words the boarding schools had forbade, then demanded to buffalo the Germans and Japanese and secure victory over Japan.

Between phases of her life, today's the day. Whatever she's crossed the country for, here it is, big as forever. Fat raindrops thwack the windshield out of nowhere, and she powers the windows down, breathes May rain in the desert summertime, narcotic and healing and right.

Alone on the highway north, save for a black semi that blows by, a woman driving, looked like.

She holds a breath from one marker to the next, only the slightest tingle of guilt this time—for what?—lets it loose, dizzy and alive.

Crosses the bridge.

Drives into a dirt yard, two dogs laying under a blue truck.

A kid with Daddy's blue eyes stood just inside the screen door she'd worked her way up to knocking on. He looked her in the face, smiled, the corner chipped off one of his front teeth. From inside came a drumbeat and the smell of cornbread and sage, a gust of air with a taste to it. Piece of paper where he'd written the address folded in her fingers.

"Somebody's here," he said. The kid drummed air with two red sticks.

"Who?"

The second voice was a woman's. And the third was her own, her puny voice speaking. Jack said they trained Mormon missionaries how to cold knock on a door, to smile, not too much. How to find a common thread—weather, the paint color, dogs. There he was, waiting.

Blue eyed, drumming. Drummer Hoff fired it off.

"Hi," she said. "Does Mr. Paris live here?"

The screen door was busted out on bottom, oily looking. Squealed on its hinges. "I'm Louie," he said, rat-tat-tatted the wood frame.

"That's my dad's middle name."

"Maybe we're related."

"Maybe we are," she said.

A big smiling woman appeared behind him. The drumbeat ceased. With her came the cornbread smell, how he'd make it with buttermilk and fresh eggs, dice jalapeño and onion, slather the cut wedges with salted butter. They ate it for dessert in Utah, so he'd always say, *I come from a place where we don't eat cornbread for dessert,* sometimes out of the blue, his punchline.'

"That's a pretty car," the smiling woman said. "I'm Big Rose. Little Rose is out back."

If you need to turn loose of, take to Edgar T. Parris in Dinnehotso, AZ, the address printed in his professor handwriting. A whole bunch of American cars leak oil on the grassless yard, and it's a Tuesday. Hadn't he written a whole chapter about how the world will never end on a Tuesday?

"It's an Outback. I had a blowout at the state line."

Big Rose props the busted-out screen open with a rock, steps outside. Arizona or Utah?

"New Mexico."

Who must be Little Rose is in the doorway now, and an Indian kid who must be the same age as blue-eyed Louie. He's got a basketball, dribbles right there on the floor.

"Why sweetie," Big Rose said with her butter-melt smile, "what on earth you doing in New Mexico?"

Where were the trees? That's what you noticed when you drove cross country from east to west, how the trees disappeared and the ground dried up, and even in May everything seemed to die, so people would say there's nothing there but empty space, which was the furthest thing from truth.

"I'm Luce," Luce said. "I've been trying to get here."

Now there were four faces catching light on the front porch that was no front porch at all.

"Why on earth would you want to get *here?*"

A man stepped through the door, scraggly pony tail and earth eyes. "I've been asking myself that all day, Rosie."

"Shut up, Lynyrd. Nobody ast you."

Didn't look to have rained here, maybe not ever, certainly not much. Bright sun in her face from the west. She should crack the Sube windows. Too hot and the Indian rosewood might crack, the Sitka spruce. Why didn't those dogs under the leaky cars bark?

"My father left me instructions," Luce said. "To come here."

Big Rose made a sign to the man she'd called Lynyrd, and he lit a cigarette between his lips, passed it to her.

"What for?"

"22,004 East and 40,000 South. That's what it said on your mailbox."

"Big numbers," a third Indian woman said, walking out to join them. "I'm Mama Linda Watchtower." She tapped index and middle fingers to her sunglasses. "Keeping an eye out," she said.

Which one of them was she supposed to be speaking to? Surely they trained the Mormons to focus their dialogue on dogs and paint colors and weather with only one soul at a time.

"It's the distance to the Temple, hon. That's what happened to all our addresses out here, they got stretched."

A blue Monte Carlo rolls up the dirt drive, a dust devil whirling up the grown-over ditch between yard and highway.

"That's my daughter, Rita," Big Rose said.

"I've had a lot of time to think about it. In miles, I mean." Luce held up the slip of paper with Daddy's handwriting on it.

"It's a lot of miles out here," Lynyrd said.

Big Rose told him to shut up again. He must be her husband. Rita got out of the Monte Carlo, held a hand above her eyes like she was saluting the whole bunch of them.

"Rita Begay," she said. That smile.

"Luce Harvell."

A white face shone where the screen door had been. She'd seen it before, Luce, in another world and time. Where there were trees green with the life of living things. She didn't know it but she had. And the man had beheld her as well, had slept in her basement, her father's accomplice in crime.

"I see," Rita said. "Come on in."

And they joined together at a table lardered with frybread and butter, meats and cheese and a kind of jelly made out of choke cherries. Ice water and coffee and Lynyrd sneaked a beer. Luce was hungry and the food was good, and they spoke not a word of the reason for her visit, nor that they took her arrival to be the sign they'd awaited, had prayed for on the very day.

Help us.

Translate the mystery.

Please.

Have pity.

And then thank you. Most of all, thank you.

They ate like there was no tomorrow, into the dusky night that breathed life into Monument Valley in the distance, Valley of the Gods, Bears Ears and Sleeping Ute, Mule Ear and the San Juan. Nor did they speak of the dynamite writ with the names of the dead, nor of Stoner, how he sought word of Paris. She did not tell them that about her father, nor the Martin D-28 in the backseat of the Sube. Or of Mama, way off in Florida. What happened to Daddy. The frybread just kept on coming, Mama Linda laughing her goofy Indian laugh, the boy named Yazzie and the other Louie of the blue eyes. There was honey and poor man's jelly, and the jam of sweet choke cherry. It became clear that Luce would spend a night in the house built on space stretched out from a far-off temple, that whatever business they all had together could wait till tomorrow, and the brand-new day. A cobbler appeared, vanilla ice cream and the smell of coffee.

When they stepped outside to smoke, the sky blasted in every direction, lit by the stars and planets and interstellar dust that composed their blood and bone. "Get those away," Rose told Louie, pointed at his red drumsticks.

Smoke rose, prayer, and the oneness of the cosmos rained down onto the lands of the woolly-headed Washers.

15.

But he won't fail today, will he, Stoner. A fine, hot Humpday, he cruises over Greasewood Flat to the Dinnehotso Chapter House, crosses the dilapidated bridge over Laguna Creek, and the schoolhouse where they'd buried the girl's birth sack, so it would be the center of her universe, and she'd return to teach and be a role model for the next generation. Rose Begay, first of her people to darken the door of a University, Miss Native American University of Utah, an Honors student like Joanna'd been, she did come back, with a diploma and teaching certificate. People were proud of her, she was queen of the Bluff Rodeo Parade and the governor had made her honorary ambassador for the State of Utah. She'd been to D.C., was an emissary at the U.N. headquarters in New York City. It was all over the papers, Rose Begay. And with all that opportunity handed to her on a goddamn silver platter, she'd had the great good sense to hook up with the sort of man, an Arkie, no less, who'd pull old cholly out in broad daylight on a federal monument and piss on a holy man of god. It was just too much, wasn't it? And for Joanna—why couldn't he get shed of her?—to insinuate that she'd done the same thing, thrown it all away for him, defied all that was good and right about their union. He'd married her in the Temple for Jesus sake. The goddamn Temple. They were consecrated. Sealed. Belonged to each other for eternity.

For her to put Stoner on the level of that Arkie, she deserved to live in Vernal with crackheads and dopers and Dino-land. Didn't she?

The truck he's looking for sits right there. In a dirt front yard with a dog sleeping under it. Bright and shine, come to papa. He's tempted to turn on the gumball machine, let the siren wail, wake the Indians in a good way, how he'd once done hitchhikers whose sleeping bags were unrolled right on the roadside, wake up and piss, boy, the world's on fire.

He doesn't exactly have a warrant. Not exactly.

There's the three-year-old expired one. Signed by Judge Rasmussen in Flag. Not binding. The old business with defacing a Book of Mormon in a Detention Facility, he'd never really written it up, so that wouldn't hold water. There was no law he could think of against shacking up with an Indian girl, or was there? He'd have to check, Stoner. With Arkies, all you had to do was sniff around some, something would show, wouldn't it.

In North Carolina, before he got fired as a missionary, a dark-haired beauty who'd slipped him her phone number had made a cut about his underwear, right in front of Dusty. The Temple garments everyone had to wear day and night, and only take off for special occasions, like you know what. She'd called them *Jesus jammies*, their garments, asked if it was true. About their bodies being temples capable of things beyond belief when exulted to holiness. Was what she'd heard about all that real?

Not exactly an Arkie, the girl with her silly question, but close enough. He didn't make the rules, Stoner, what Jo could never get through her hard head. Wasn't him made her keep the garment vow and the rest.

Truth is, he's wearing garments this second, clean and fresh against his skin, and if he's not bullet proof, he is shielded by the fabric of God, so how about that?

The dogs go into conniptions when he drives onto the dirt yard, kills it so the motor ticks a few times before he gets out.

They're not chained, Indian dogs, never were. And everybody and their mother knows he's here now, don't they? Might as well get to it, might as well.

They'd had two whole days of training back in Provo on how to deal with dogs, him and Dusty. Given they'd always be walking two-by-two through neighborhoods where there would certainly be unleashed dogs, it was important to work as a team, to identify a situation before it happened, to carry treats and know words the canines wanted to hear—*biscuit, walk, good dog*. Never turn your back on one, a loose dog. Stand your ground, but don't push. Look it in the eye, the dog, unlike a bear or big cat. Make yourself big, the two of you together. Say the words. Give it a piece of jerky. Name it and own it. And if the treats and words and making yourself big didn't work, kick the shit out of the son of a bitch, and climb a tree if one is available. Unlike bears and cats, dogs couldn't climb trees, most of them.

Be the boss.

Stoner stepped out of the patrol car, left the door open. They were mongrels, both of them, related by blood, probably, and one of them was going ape shit, barking like it was about to explode, but the other, the heavier of the two, just stared, a low growl in its throat.

That's the one to watch. Quiet boy with the low snarl.

"Good dog," Stoner said. "Want a biscuit?"

He held a hand out, palm up, pretended to taste the biscuit, smack-smacking and chewing it, offering it to the pointy-eared barker, collarless, hadn't had its shots, no doubt.

"King," Stoner said. "Josh. Spinky. Satan."

Nope.

"Want to go for a walk?"

The quiet one has one blue eye, one black, obsidian and sky. That low growl. They've split up, the barker from behind, and the one that wants to bite his ass crouched in front.

He unsnaps his pistol latch, something he'd never had as a missionary, a sidearm, though he wished it a million times. Still, hard to hit a moving dog at close range, not like the movies, not at all.

He'd been bit, more than once. His mother's brother, Uncle Earl, had sicced a Labrador retriever on him at Lake Powell. Just about the moment he ran off a cliff with a rope swing in his hand, so the dog had grabbed hold of his left foot and swung off with him, hung on till they hit water, then clawed his back trying to swim out. It had got infected, the dog bite, and he'd never said sorry or kiss my ass or anything at all, Uncle. What was wrong with the Lees?

The quiet one means business. He's the one. Indians always have at least one mean son of a bitch to watch their backs. Giving Stoner the evil eye, the growl low and real.

"Get!" Stoner says.

It bares teeth, the dog.

"I said Get!" Stoner said again.

Try bossing somebody else's dog around if you want to know how important you are, how much heft your words really have. Supposed to be, he'd have a canister of pepper spray on his holster, but supposed to be was back in the old world, before he'd holed up at Jacob's Lake for a month of Sundays, mourning Joanna and the black plague, how he never seemed to get things right. The dog could smell it on him, his failures. It was payback time. And payback's hell.

The other time was when he was serving a divorce notice on a man who'd unlatched his door, opened it wide, said *skit*. He remembers how the K was hard against the roof of the man's mouth, who was about to lose his wife and kid and car all in one foul blow.

"Skit," he said.

It stopped. The growl dead in its throat.

He could feel the one in back, not a tree from here to the

cottonwoods on Laguna Creek. Coming at him two at once. The Arkie's truck close enough to spit on—he could hop the bumper, climb up on the bed, get up on the cab if he had to. And how would that look to the Indians inside, Stoner on top of Paris's truck cab? No, he wouldn't fail today. Shoot them both if he had to, but he wasn't going to run. Not today.

The one who wanted his ass took notice. Dogs are like that. They can tell when you decide. Arkansas DMF 936. Dumb mother fucker. Tags are expired. Silver Subaru. 2005, something like that. Outback. Florida plates. The sunshine state. Who on earth drives a Subaru to the Rez from Florida?

Someone whistled, low then high. Over to the shed.

The dogs up and ran.

Then the explosion, and the world caught fire.

16.

Coca-Cola first went on sale this week in Atlanta, Georgia, 1886, had real cocaine in it Louie the Washer kid said, and he ought to know, all the people with his blood served time. John Deere died a week later. Racehorse Winning Brew ran a quarter mile in twenty seconds, and Astronomer John Herschel—who was really a horn player in a symphony—died in 1871. Rain caused a deadly sinkhole in some town Lynyrd can't pronounce and *kindnesses are like grain, they increase with sewing.* Lynyrd doesn't get the last bit, increase with sewing, but notes that today is the 125th day of the year, and the full moon's on the 26th, when a lunar eclipse will be seen throughout North America. Back in the general classified, SISTER LIGHT still advertises out of Spartanburg, South Carolina, and Spiritual Healer Helen P. from Egypt claims to *clear stumbling blocks and stop all root work.* Root work? For some reason Big Rose buys him *The New Old Farmer's Almanac* first thing every Christmas, and he's usually read half of it before New Years. "Useful, with a pleasant degree of humor," how it describes itself—true enough. Where on earth else could you go from the planet being at perigee to Mama Sophia Redhand, under whose phone number is written DON'T TELL ME, I'LL TELL YOU.

He reads the tiny print in the bathroom mornings before light, and the chores that take him out to the chicken coop with the slop bucket from last night. He has to water the strawberries, and dead patch of grass Big Rose claims still lives, hit the plants in pots on the back porch, and check to make sure the well house pumps aren't clogged and on the verge of exploding again. He'll pick whatever lettuce hasn't burnt to hell, and maybe there's a spring onion or radish.

Best to do the work before the heat comes on. And there's the thing about being the only one up when the light's just coming, hot coffee and, this morning, the big planet Jupiter riding the crescent moon's shoulder.

The Harvell girl'd come, though they're not sure why. Something to do with bird man, birdy, bird, bird. He's made the coffee strong, the way he likes it, and will no doubt start the old, old fight with Big R, or a last blow on the coals. And this morning, this one in particular, 3rd of May, clear with the conjunction and juniper in the air, there's the feel of anticipation, SISTER LIGHT out there working her mojo, Mama Sophia, and the earth at perihelion—or was it apogee. Aphelion? There's a little Astronomical Glossary up front before the Dr. Rototiller and Burn Safely and Stand Up Straight and Feel Better advertisements, tells you all you need to know about Golden Numbers and Magnitude, which was furthest away and which was closest.

Aphelion, for sure, come July, Dog Days.

His grandmother, who'd give him the Navajo name he couldn't pronounce, once told him that, at 86, she didn't feel any different whatsoever than when she was sixteen. Maybe her joints and muscles, some, but not in what mattered, what was inside her heart. She died in September. He'd visited her room and sprinkled blue sage from the Abajo, and cedar, like she'd asked. The room had smelled like lizard. He remembered that, lizard.

"What you call yourself Lynyrd for," she'd asked. "Say?"

All these people coming in and out of your life like waves.

She'd made fun of him for it, Big Rose, not being able to say his name. "I could teach you, you know."

"No thank you."

"How come?"

The sun turned Comb Ridge the color of a pork chop, with streaks of fat and bone, a touch of white gravy and the blue bowl of sky. How about them apples? Hang your hat on that. The teachers at Indian School had told him he was stupid. You're just a stupid Indian boy, that's all, get over it, you have to live your life, stupid or not. For a long time, he believed them. Maybe he still did. Big Rose certainly thought him so, most of the time, she did.

In the morning, when it got light, Lynyrd was plenty happy to be Lynyrd, and did not feel in the least like a stupid Indian boy. Shaved-headed Kennard had taught him how to play "Tuesday's Gone With The Wind" on slide guitar, a little hog nose amp and a Fender with a busted little E string. It had a sadness that touched his soul, and when Ronnie Van Zandt sang "my baby's gone with the wind," you believed it through and through. No faking that kind of pain, how he'd felt when Grandmother Maryboy had give up the ghost in that liz-ard-smelling room, and he was left with the shell in his mouth of a word he couldn't say.

This morning he thinks to pray.

It's easy, really. You just say something like great mystery, thank you for this day. Help me that I might do the right thing. Be with Big Rose and don't let her be so mean. Help those kids who dug up dynamite buried in Big Cave 1, and don't let them blow themselves and everyone else to smithereens. Help those chickens, pecking each other raw. Why they peck so much? What's wrong with them? Be with our ancestors and let them know we think of them. Who'd prayed us through seven gener-ations. Protect them from Covid, and don't let the well explode again. Take care of our water. Help Rose translate the mystery of green and growing things. Let them know what to do with those those named sticks with their wire fuses. The Unknown one. Help that girl find whatever it is she's looking for. Be with Grandmother Mary and Nephew Yazz, those people Mama Linda'd swindled, so they weren't so pissed they'd call the cops.

He didn't shut his eyes when he prayed, just went about his business. And just when the hard *p* of *cops* came off his lips, a cruiser with its lights off pulled through the gap in the grown over fence, right into the yard where the tracks looked like italics, what you did when you underlined a word to make it stronger.

Stoner.

Sat there a minute. Got out the car. Pistol on his hip. Unsnapped holster.

Only Thelma and Louise weren't having any of it. Not one bit. The former yip-yapping at his heels, while the latter put the fear of God into him with her silence from the front. That's how it looked, fear of God.

He finished the prayer as he always did, said *thank you*. Though he was never entirely sure, Lynyrd, who was *you*. Sometimes it felt like *he* was *you*, though he hadn't figured why you'd pray to yourself.

For the kingdom of God is within you.

Who was *you*?

Seven eggs clicked in the little bucket. You could tell which pecker laid each by its color, light brown for the Sex Links, darker for the Rhode Island Reds. Stoner looks like he's about to jump up on his car, hasn't seen him yet. He touches the gun butt, Louise crouched not ten feet in front of him. People in the house sleeping, except Rita, maybe, about to drive to the bridge and sell mojos. Big Rosie snoring on her side of the bed, the pillow dented, a little wet. Edgar and Little Rose, had the boys walked home? The Harvell girl, Lucy she'd named herself.

He couldn't search the house, could he?

Lynyrd whistled. A low note going high.

Said, *here.*

Thelma and Louise came. They were good dogs. You could talk to them and they'd listen. If there were just more people like that.

The noise came from nowhere.

Both dogs yelped. For a second, Lynyrd thought he'd shot them.

He dropped the egg bucket, hit the ground. There was some of them, the Indian boys, who'd gone off to war and got shot. Older kids sent to the jungle lands overseas, some of whom came back in uniforms and marched in the rodeo parade with their outfits decorated, bright medals on their chests. Not Lynyrd.

He'd not been shot at.

And wouldn't today, didn't look like. Stoner's put both hands to his ears, hit the dirt. Not yet seven o'clock on a Wednesday morning, dark coffee in the little Italian expresso maker on the stove, a stack of leftover frybread wrapped in foil on top of the fridge.

And the quiet after the noise.

They hadn't gone home, the boys. Yazz and Louie, who'd brought the shit back from BC[1], Unknown written on the three. Now Stoner was privy, and whatever happened next was not likely to be something any of them had ever wanted for the first Wednesday in May 2021, Mother's Day just around the corner, Monument Valley Graduation, Air Balloon Days over in Bluff.

And he'd dropped the egg bucket.

Big Rosie'd kick his ass.

It dawns on him that she could be hurt, that an accident has happened, the house blown up, maybe, someone killed, a gas explosion, something with the TNT, that about everyone he loved in the world was in that house, and he'd best get up out of the dirt and help if he could. How these moments come at you out of the blue, and you'd best keep your head. That he loved Big Rose deeply and with a full heart, and that he could not imagine life without her and the goodness of the routine that buoyed his life.

Lynyrd got up, retrieved the egg bucket, and made his way to the front door, a little afraid of what he might find inside. Something they hadn't counted on had happened. The Harvell girl, Lucy, she was in there. Mama Linda and the boys. Rita and Edgar and Big Rosie. They planned on fried eggs and hashbrowns and hot buttered frybread. There was orange juice in the fridge, half a watermelon.

Stoner followed.

Out of the corner of his eye, Lynyrd saw the blue movement.

17.

In her dream, they called him from the beach. After the mammoth drive from Salt Lake when the air had gone out just as they hit Nebraska, and they'd had to find a shop in Sidney to have the unit recharged. To Kansas City and Nashville, where they'd toured the Country Music Hall of Fame and saw the Martin D-28 Johnny Cash had given to a young Bob Dylan, and Cash was from Arkansas, wasn't he, and they sang "Blowing in the Wind" and "I Walk the Line." Highway 10 across North Florida through Jacksonville and Ponte Vedra to St. Augustine, where they'd rented on Vilano Beach, the heat unbearable and water hot as a bathtub. Through Melbourne and Vero and West Palm to Boynton, where her earthly belongings remained in a third-floor apartment. Seven full days it had taken them to cross the country. And that last day, through the Cuban part of town to the exact line that separated public from private, the glassy water a holy blue, fishing boats rocking on the horizon. In the dream, they'd dialed his number and he'd answered, asked what they were having for dinner, did it come a thunder and lightning storm every afternoon?

The strange bed's not really a bed, taste of last night's food in her mouth, and the end of the dream ripping through her, as if dreams might take breath and roar to life.

It had rained in Utah, he'd said. Everything turned green when the sun came out.

The house had shaken. She believed the house had shaken.

There'd been an earthquake.

A sound. She was wide awake. And it comes on Luce that she's left the Martin D-28 in her Sube overnight. And now some kind of hell on wheels storm has hit, with her on a floor pallet, in a doorless room she'd never seen by daylight.

Goddamn, somebody said. Next room over. *Son of a bitch.*

Then the dogs came busting through the screen door, Lynyrd, Big Rose's husband behind them, and a dark-haired man in a police-blue uniform in chase. All this in ten seconds of waking. Not even long enough to shake off the urge to go back to sleep, realign with the dream, her and mom, the Florida beach on the day it rained in Utah.

One of the dogs drinks water, big loud slurps and backsplash.

"*Thelma*," a woman says. Mama Linda? "*Stay.*"

Her phone says seven something. The sun's out, it was neither storm nor earthquake. The explosion. Gas? No smell. Her sleeping bag on the pallet, grains of desert sand at the feet. Getting up in a strange house after an explosion doesn't seem right, like she needs permission.

Lynyrd walks by her, the dogs. Someone's knocking at the front door, *knock, knock, knock*. Just like she had yesterday, I'm looking for Mr. Edgar Paris.

Lynyrd says, "Excuse me." Goes out the sliding glass door to an arbor-covered back porch.

Then everyone's up, and she stuffs her bag into its sack—she hadn't really planned this far. Big Rose's at the stove, checking connections, shaking her head, making a sound in her throat. Mama Linda and Rita, Edgar in tighty-whities. A police man standing outside the busted out screen.

"Anybody home?" he says.

There were boys, Yazzie and the blue-eyed one.

"What in the world was that?" Big Rose's robe has roses on it, of course it would.

Mama Linda is the Indian boy's mother. She turns her back

to the front door, says, "Don't you know?"

"No."

"Yes."

"No?"

"*Yes.*"

Knock, knock, knock.

"Anybody home?"

"Will you answer that." She was looking at her, Big Rose.

She sees his eyes. They're dark. And not friendly, gazing at Luce Harvell like he knows her reason for being here, assessing her, how she fits.

Edgar's put on pants, thank God. Him and Rita go out the back door, just like that.

She hasn't even told him about the guitar, not yet. Strange that it wouldn't have come up at dinner, but it didn't. The good food. And they'd known Dad. Liked him.

Like they'd been waiting for her, how it seemed.

The D-28 had seemed secondary, like the apartment back at Boynton Beach on the other side of the continent, the other side of her brain, thunder and lightning and the thing before.

"You'll never believe," he'd told her. It was the last of their beach call, the one she'd been dreaming. Wild sunflowers had burst up outside his study window, the little room he'd built onto the back of their house, where he'd once spent mornings before light digging into the history that had marched the Pioneer Trail from Arkansas, traced the Ogallala to the North Platte, the way him and Mom had come so many years before.

They caught fire when the sun hit them.

For all her life, he'd taken a picture of her standing beside sunflowers on the first day of school. *Hardy Sunflower*, her Indian name.

They'd burst into bloom where they'd never been. In the dream, they had.

"Can I help you?" she said to the man at the door.

He stared. "I don't know," he said. "Can you?"

The boys have all run off. After the one had gone off by accident—who on earth would believe you could wet-light the fuse—and the cop showed up, and Big Rose was about to tear them all a new one, they'd hauled butt. There was a place they knew to hide, where almost no one ever went.

Almost no one, a name for the ages.

18.

The girl's face is enough like its father's, so Stoner knows the score in nothing flat. Thinks he does. Well, part of it. Those dogs had given him the willies, that quiet mongrel one. If him and Jo'd had a kid would it have looked like him? Her? Both of them mixed together? Would the Lee gene he carried be dominant, so the child would know its kith and kin, one world to the next? Would the uppity part of Jo rear its head so the kid would smart-off to its elders, get fired as a missionary like him, or would the double-whammy of both their sass cancel out the trait like happened in numbers? Would he be able to gauge her love by the way Joanna treated the child, the way it sometimes happened? Would he be odd man out? If they could raise a child into a good person, did that make *them* good people?

She'd be the driver of the Subaru with Florida plates, the girl with her father's look about her who'd just asked if she can help. Why Florida? What's in Florida for Arkies?

"I'm responding to a disturbance hereabouts," he said, not exactly true. "Do you have any information about such?" Stoner re-snapped his pistol holster, took out the little notebook with the ink pen stuck through its spiral wire.

"I don't live here," the girl said.

"Neither do I."

"Officer Stoner," Big Rose said, filling the doorway. "Morning."

He wrote the day's date down on a blue line, 5.3.21, they

added up to eleven, the numbers. Lucky. They teach you to be aware of the seven directions, the bishops up in Provo, to know what's in front of you and behind, on either side, up and down, and, most importantly, inside.

"Morning Miss Begay."

"This is Lucy. She's visiting."

"From Florida," Stoner said.

"Driving through."

"To where?"

"Can I get you a cup?" Big Rose said. "Lynyrd's made it strong today."

Rita Begay poked on her phone by the back sliding glass where the boys had run. Out where the sound came from. Where the dogs went. There was a smell, something he remembered.

"Can I ask you what just happened?"

The Arky girl with Florida plates backed off, so it was all Rose, Rita and the Watchtower woman backing her up. "You don't get by here much," Rose said. "Firecracker, I think. Kids up to no good."

The one they call Yazzie'd been here, slick basketball he dribbled wherever he went, on the floor by the sliding glass, a fall hazard.

"I don't think that was a firecracker, Rose."

She let the words settle. "You here as a policeman, or a person?"

"Are the two different animals?"

It had been an explosion. Gasoline or bomb, maybe. Dumb ass Arkie playing with homemade bombs. No, he'd run out in his underwear. Not even the Arkie was that stupid. Yazzie. Some of his dirt bag hoodlum homies?

"They wake us up sometimes."

They?"

A liar's voice gives them away, the slight rise, difference in air intake, the tendency to talk fast. Rose was an elder, related to old Sun Bear who'd known his great grandfather. Didn't drink. Voted. A decent Indian. Save letting her Miss Utah Native American granddaughter take up with that Arkie convict.

"Kids," she said. "You catch'em, you tan their hides."

Didn't miss a beat, Rose. He smelled the coffee, the other thing. They were getting away, whoever'd run.

"The truck with Arkansas plates parked in your front yard has expired tags. I could ask to see the registration," Stoner said.

"If you're here as a cop."

Stoner made a question mark after the date. Joanna'd said the same thing to him one time—you here as a cop or a man?

"I'm not," Stoner said. "I was just driving by, sounded like all hell broke loose. Somebody could be hurt, whatever you're blowing up back there."

Rita handed a cup of steaming coffee through the busted screen—he'd questioned her already, seen her mojos.

On her way to work, sashayed right on by with a backpack and a water jug. "See you at the bridge," she said, started her junker Chevy and drove away, and it was only later, when he'd thought about it and wrote the details in his little spiral note-book, that he thought she'd driven the wrong way. Toward Utah and Monument Valley, and not toward Lee's Ferry at all.

Written under the date with its crooked question mark. Was he a cop or a person? Couldn't you be both?

"Will there be anything else, Roger?"

Harvell, his name had been, the girl's father. A professor up in Salt Lake. History. Hadn't it been him who wrote the letter for Joanna and that trip to France she'd always regretted not taking? The one he'd needled her with, "Oh yeah, you've got verve and common sense, Jo, boatloads." Said, "As a person, you are humorous, kind, and bold."

What was *verve*, anyway? What kind of person said that? Not all it was cracked up to be, he bet.

He'd cold-knocked a thousand doors up through that

morning. Had looked into the faces of mothers who'd just learned their sons had died in car wrecks. He'd preached the gospel of Jesus Christ, accepted illicit phone numbers, served warrants and divorce papers. He'd said that *no, he didn't want to be kicked in the balls first. Would there be anything else, Roger?*

"Yeah, Miss Begay," he said. "You tell Edgar Paris his tags are expired. And if I see him driving, I'll pull his ass over, and it ain't going to be pretty."

She smiled through the screen. Out came a whiff of frybread. The mug burned in his right hand.

"Will do," she said.

She said it in a way that meant goodbye, sir, our business is done. He'd been sent away from front porches and doorsteps all across North Carolina in the same way, only southerners had this way of damning you to hell in a sweet way. "Why bless your heart," they'd say. Or, "Isn't that something." His bench warrant was expired, by a long shot. There was no law against white co-habitating with Indians though there should be. He ought to have a word with the Florida girl, see how she just happens to be here in the thick of things.

The front door shuts in front of his face. Locks.

They're up to something, sure as shit. Kids my ass. Whatever went off out behind the house meant business. The men had left pretty fast out the back door. Stoner could sniff out rat from a mile away. Ratty-rat-rat.

And she hadn't turned in the right direction for Marble Canyon, had she, Rita Begay. It was all somehow related—the Harvell girl looking so like her daddy. Paris. The truck with expired tags, under which slept that dog from hell. Blowing something up behind the house. Bomb-making. Big Rose lying straight to his face. The Watchtower woman crooked as a stick. Yazzie leaving his basketball to roll on the floor, some of his hooligan homies in there somewhere. Rita driving the wrong way. *Hmmm.*

Yep, Stoner smelled rat alright.

And there was something else. Joanna was somehow part of this. How Big Rose's words came straight out of his ex's mouth: *You here as a cop or a man?* Of being two things at once. Driving away from the Begay dirt yard, onto the blacktop toward Mexican Water and Snake House Mesa over to Bluff where his people'd been sent by Brigham Young himself, and had they ever suffered from that trip. Had they ever. The last of it with the oxen down on bloody knees, over San Juan Hill to Bluff where everything they ever built was flooded, and the cemetery overlooking town was testament to their everlasting travail. There'd been Lees among them, always willing to do the prophet's bidding. To serve the Lord God no matter the hardship.

The land was big and it opened up before him. Rita Begay out there, Paris and Miss Native American Utah, Lynyrd whose name was not Lynyrd, the kids, and the Harvell girl. He'd have to run her particulars, dig up whatever there was to dig.

Too long in a hole, he's clear-headed for the first time since. Sees Mama Linda Watchtower sneak off down the creek bank, running for the beat-up trailer where they'd arrested her sweet thing all those years back, sent him to the pen.

Hoe-down, be damned.

That Mama Linda, always stirring the shit.

19.

The story gets told over and over, its parts circled back on, some-times this one stressed, sometimes the other. Kidding's heard it all, seen a good bit. No kidding. Of all, the one that gets his goat, sticks in his crawl so that she seeps through his dreams, the seams of his waking sewn to the dark place behind the cave mouth, hard pack where he'd first felt her pull on his heart and mind and, yes, spirit to the place where she lay immaculate, a slight incline on the flat stone, in her right arm the mummified child laced to the cradle board, and at her throat the painted face and bobbed hair of what he'd named—as a much younger man who'd yet to learn the power of love medicine—her *trophy*. The place so seared into his psyche that written into his final will and testament were instructions for his own interment on a little rise overlooking the creek and Kinboko Canyon, Skeleton Mesa on the horizon. And what a word that was, *inter*, the deposit of human remains he'd so world famously mined, the chief necromancer of his time. Dragging its Latin trainload of baggage: situated or occurring in between. But between where and where, exactly? Because at its core, the *here* implies a *there*. And to *disinter*, wouldn't that be to rob the human soul of *there*? Mother and child and whatever in the name of God that thing tied to her neck was supposed to stand for? He'd be in the ground some thirty years when they brought her back for reburial, only not there, in Big Cave One, with its atlatls and painted dots and white dog mummies. What would they make of that back at Harvard? Alfonzo Vance Kidding sewn with yucca thread into a two-piece woven shroud and laid beneath the very dirt he'd so meticulously removed from the mouths and nostrils, the ear canals he'd sent on trains to the Peabody on the other edge of the continent? Between *where* and *where*?

Her *trophy*, he'd called it in the paper. The scalp.

An easy enough mistake.

The Plains Indians took them in warfare, power symbols of victory hung on sticks and marched into battle celebrations, laced into the manes of horses reined onto the war path. And if you followed that trail far enough, wouldn't it march right down from the Dakotas into Wyoming and the Colorado Plateau, down Ratton Pass into the south and west, to Tesegi with its forever of dry caves where the Basketmakers sought shelter and kindled fire, buried their kin in unmarked cists with games and food and dogs and babies and whatever magic to propel them from here to there. For there must be a there, as here was certainly proof. And they weren't so different, were they, the Basketmakers from Kidding's people. They were born, had mothers and fathers, uncles and aunts, got hungry and sick, were happy sometimes. They loved and were loved, and isn't that what separates us, finally, from the rest? The capacity to love?

And they died and got buried, were remembered and then forgotten.

The same old story that gets repeated, sometimes this stressed and sometimes the other.

And the archeology of the Southwest was in its infancy when Kidding first camped Chinle Wash on the San Juan, just above Mule Ear, the volcanic throat that had spewed the alluvial fan with garnet and slag, so the anthills shone in the moonlight that October when he was twenty-four and the cottonwoods had turned yellow before the night of first frost. Water was frozen in the dish bucket next morning, a glass-thin pane. Sun shone on the folds of Raplee Anticline, so it seemed the world's ribs were showing, not ten miles from Sand Island outside Bluff, with its Sixteen Room Ruin and swinging bridge. Where they'd spent a night at Recapture and heard the stories from a Navajo woman who'd married Apache, and knew the trail up Chinle past Poncho House, all the way to Canyon de Chelly where Kit Carson had burned the orchards and marched a whole slew of them to Oklahoma before the Reservation came into being. You can walk that trail clear to Second Mesa, the woman said, south and west to Kayenta and Marsh Pass—Indian Highway, she called it.

Indian highway.

Comb Ridge jutting its elephant back for eighty solid miles north and south, with only the gap at San Juan Hill where the Mormons had crossed over. Piddly ass gap, not three-hundred yards wide, first break in eighty miles, and that's where they'd found the bones, wooly mammoth, sloth and camel. Clovis and Folsom points, haft-axes knapped for chopping big-boned prey, twin petroglyphs on a panel face, bifurcated trunks curled from block bodies. The sons-of-a-bitches had ambushed elephants here, and though tree ring dating was not yet certain, and radio carbon was a million miles off, they knew enough about the late Pleistocene fauna to judge these hunters as kin to those who'd walked the land bridge from Siberia, down the Puget Sound and sweeping left turn into the Columbia Gorge and left again on the Salmon, and some had made their way here for the slaughter and extinction event that sent them packing.

Ten thousand years ago. Maybe twenty.

And who would have thought that these Basketmakers, whose caves had been trespassed by cliff dwellers and Puebloans, Tewa and Zuni, who could have guessed they'd walked here from the south, Mesoamerica, distinct, sharing little to nothing with the ancient hunters? They'd worked backwards at Harvard and Princeton and everywhere else. They all had it ass backward. They'd come from the south, the Basketmakers, before Christ, bearing the corncobs and metate stones of Mexico, the feathered serpent God and flesh consuming religion, ritual cannibalism and inducting their enemies into the tribe via the scalp ceremony, the elaborate curation of such as rainmakers and caretakers, who'd weep before the rains came and, when chewed by holy women and spit to make cakes, could cure longing and make one brave. They would speak at night and warn of danger, and one with a face and lips, the delicate eyelashes and brows intact, hair tied in perfect lobes over each ear, such would be a mighty protector, no?

It wasn't a trophy. Or if it was, not the kind he'd meant, Kidding.

But of course he knew not one lick of this that morning after first frost, when the light fell down on Raplee Anticline and he first walked the Chinle up out of the alluvial fan into the canyon.

Where his life was turned in another direction, and what he sought was what he found—a there to get to from here.

Wild donkeys, remnants of the Spanish who came here seeking gold and the souls of this New Spain, have cut a trail into the canyon along the creek, just south and east with Mule Ear diatreme taking the sky in one direction, and blue sky riding earth's backbone to the other. Across hills of cobble that mark the riverbed's migration, the occasional yellow cottonwood golden and smoking with its roots sunk down in the mirror image of its limbs. Far off on the cliff faces and infolds, shelters, rock work, the craft of human hands plain at a distance. The ancient enemy would see, know he walked into land lived on across ages. With him, the other greenbacks Peabody'd sent to walk the wash, chase rumors of a point workshop and pottery kiln, a pool of clay with the perfect ration of quartz to silt, the flute player with dangling phallus, a supposed Basketmaker power symbol overlaid with Navajo medicine. Star Woman, pregnant with star child. An Indian highway up and out of the canyon, rattlesnake glyphs and moki stairways, painted kivas and corn crypts, a Wolf Man panel, river left, the Navajo Nation. Dueling shamans with atlatls in hand.

Bear tracks gash the muddy wash.

Him and the others have to cross here and there, and then a rise before a sharp turn where literally every square foot of earth held shards: pieces of corrugated pots fired when it came to be understood that corrugations increased the volume to be heated, which in turn increased heat and so quickened the boil necessary for the Anasazi beans to unlock their protein, to simmer ground corn into mush for cakes. Painted pieces, Mancos black on white ticked triangles, Cortez, elaborate lines of interlocked scrolls. Handles and rims and Abajo Red on Orange. The stray human tooth. The stuff was everywhere, impossible not to step on. Here on a piddly rise not a mile from the river. Not even in the canyon yet. Heaps of wild donkey dung covering thousand-year-old ceramic wear, never seen, likely, by a white eye. They'll take some on the way out, Kidding's told.

They're burning daylight.

Walk single file to the bluff cliff face, its beginning point hidden from the river. Twenty-, thirty-feet high with talus and scree, within a rock's throw of the creek, the first corn cribs shimmer on the invisible wall, appear then disappear, seem never to have been touched since sealing. Impossible to scale without ropes, defensive looking. Made to hide. There was warfare. Competition for resources. Hunger. Much pain. And the end of it. Kidding makes note of the exact location, binding the structures with adjoining features. They move slowly. And times gets funny the way it does on site.

It was believed that certain witch-men could stop time, prevent the sun from rising, or make it rise faster. The sun shaman cult could summon rain, the thunder beings, corn from the maiden. Star Woman comes out of nowhere.

She is beautiful, outlines in white, enormous belly with a clearly delineated star inside, white, glimmering. Handprints above and below, on either side. Gazing out over the way they'd come, following bear track, scat, painted pottery.

Who they'd named Baseball Man rears on the wall patina just south. The perfect square shoulders, fine arms with clean hands at its side, the size of a man, and not one to mess with, face turned on anyone who approached—enough to turn them around. Put the fear of God in them, Kidding thinks.

Painted over the Anasazi warrior, a Navajo circle, three feet in diameter with curved lines inside just like a baseball's stitching. To take and redirect its medicine, turn it inward. Or at least take the edge off for the sheepherders who'd walk this way in fear.

Someone has laid a golden eagle at the foot of Baseball Man. A bundle of cedar tied to a painted stick. Yellow, Red, Black and White, the great eagle's talons clasp an arrow shaft, a tight-knapped point resined to the business end. Across the creek, duck-headed people, shamans in a fight to the death. Inhabited still, this place. And not for the first time nor the last, he knew he intruded, Kidding. That the spirits were pissed to the core with the Peabody boys' presence and were about to manifest themselves in wind.

Kidding takes the tobacco pouch from his day pack, undoes the slip knot, holds a fistful of the crimped leaf toward the sun, says the prayer the Navajo woman who'd married an Apache taught him. Three words, repeated. That he might do things in a good way, so the land will open itself to him, be his teacher.

That he might love and sip cool water and say thank you, and not be afraid. Walk the red road from here to there, and give back as much as he takes.

Amen.

PART TWO

20.

The light gets all funny in the desert, so that once you've been there and taken it into your brain through its windows, the eyes, there's no going back to before, even without an Indian princess whose soft breathing you wake to on a morning that might as well be earth's last day for its beauty and clean serenity and all manner of things be well, until they are not. He smells coffee. Good. Rose Marie Begay, who for a reason that is beyond him believes him to be a good man, worth the trouble, whose laugh comes sudden as wind with the notes of a raven riding on it, the sound she makes when they fly over, so a lone one will sometimes circle back, trilling, imitating the call, trying to get it right. More than once, he was certain it was her signaling him, only out of sight, the way Indians sometimes did things—Mama Rita's hog-leg under the table blanket with its eight-pointed stars to mirror the cosmos in all directions: up, down, on either side, front, back, inside, outside. Raven woman, she'd had one tattooed inside her bicep, black as the semi-truck that blew through his dreams, always headed for the cliff when Edgar woke, lungs on fire, about to explode.

He'd seen the desert. No going back.

Still May, some chill to the night. In Arkansas, you'd sweat the moment you stepped from the shower, maybe even in the shower, if that was possible. Ninety-percent humidity, people just didn't know. You forget pain like that, like a woman

111

forgets having a baby, if all that's true. How would he know. Well, how would he?

Car wheels on the gravel outside. The dogs ballistic. Thelma and Louise. Bad. But maybe not *bad*, bad. You have to give a morning a chance. Don't you? So many times in his life he'd given up too soon. But not today. Not anymore. That's what love will do for you, give you some wiggle room. Make you more than yourself. Lift you up to your proper state. Because we're all meant to be loved, aren't we? That's been his trouble all along, not seeing the truth straight in front of his face. Love.

Cigarette smoke through the opened window, boys up already, out there in back of the house, striking matches. A far off voice comes to him, speaking Russian, cursing him like a yard dog: *do not smoke, you idiot. DO NOT.*

Bad.

Rosie's been sickly of late. She'd missed her period. They've bought a pee test, only Rose was waiting for the full Flower moon, three weeks off, which doesn't really make sense to Edgar, whose mother and father were both gone now, buried half a world away, whose sister had sworn him off and whose brother'd run off to no man's land. He wasn't related to anyone else on earth he knew of in particular, save Rose, now, maybe. She was part of his story now, and it had changed, been turned toward the better out here in Indian Country, not far from the state line, Monument Valley as far as you could see. He'd unwired the bridge, done right as a free man. Took the stuff where Big Rose said, Tsegi, Big Cave One, where no one dared walk for what they'd found there eighty, a hundred years ago. A haunted place, though Edgar hadn't felt it that day they buried it, each stick with a name written in black sharpie, the last of them Unknowns, the ones the kids had pilfered, up to no good, spray-painting VIVA LAS VEGAS over the Anasazi hand prints, peeing on glyphs, digging it up. Looky here what I found. What is it, exactly. Is it bigger than a bread box? Is it a donkey's dick?

The watchtower woman getting word.

Now they wanted to see it, she had connections, the Watchtower woman. Her boy, Yazz, and that Washer kid, they'd be go betweens. Maybe get enough mula for a trip to Hawaii or something. Didn't they deserve that? Didn't they? A honeymoon in Hawaii, lay on the beach and sip Mai Tai. He didn't know exactly what a Mai Tai was, but it sure sounded good. All those hula girls on surfboards. Mount Diamond Head where Jimmy Hendrix played once, that's what Lynyrd said, he'd read about it on Wiki. Maybe enough for them all to go. But they had to make sure it still worked, didn't they?

You couldn't sell it if it didn't work.

Maybe it had got too wet, or the insides rotted. They'd never thought to try it out, him and Harvell, they'd taken the Russian's word, who'd stole it from that ginormous mine, the deepest hole dug on earth up in the Ochres. Traceable, still, hot, and if you ever touched it, some of the atoms got under your fingernails and stayed there the rest of your life Lynyrd said, he read it somewhere. Best go ahead and send the stuff somewhere else, now that the kids had sniffed it out. Linda'd set the ball to rolling. Much interest out there, she promised.

But what they needed was a test. Did it work?

Rose opened one eye, said *ugh*. The morning sickness. Cigarette smoke didn't help, coming from outside. Dog barking to beat the band. Somebody'd driven a car onto the yard.

Smell of coffee. A little chill in the air. Giving the morning a chance, what they were up to, him and Rosie, the rest.

That morning way back when, a Christmas Eve, Harvell'd told him to go on home, Edgar, he didn't have to be part of the end. Blowing the bridge could put you in the pokey for life. Sitting up on the house rock overlook, Paria Canyon, the Vermillion Cliffs just starting to shine. A fine cold morning with the sun rising. The detonator hardwired, read to roll. Just go on home, he'd said, the Harvell girl's daddy, reading what the Russian woman had written at the end of her book, the instruction manual that walked them through the whole mess, interspliced with weird snippets of poetry and recollection of life in her motherland. Stoner'd walked out on the bridge there at last of it. Whomping the Book of Mormon cover Edgar'd frisbeed from the moving truck when Harvell got him out of jail. It would have been murder, blowing it with a State Trooper out there like that. Federal offense. And they hadn't thought that part through, taking a human life. Had they? Even Stoner's. Both of them, Harvell and Edgar, from the sticks. Arkansawyers. And there was the business with John D. Lee, and how they'd made the thing a monument to him, the lone man punished for Mountain Meadows, fat man's godson, reinstated to their church, made a hero, *a man of courage and indomitable spirit and good judgement.* His blood running in Stoner's veins that hot minute on the bridge when the sun rose up and morning came.

Condors nested under the bridge.

These dinosaur-looking birds with featherless heads and necks, wings wide as a Volkswagen is long, have numbers spray painted on their shoulders. 4, 7, 9 and 10, they'd eyeballed him and Harvell the whole time while they worked, drilling and packing, running the wire. Witnesses, if anyone knew what they were up to, it was those dino-birds.

The twin bridges just catching first light. Ole Number 7 hopped a handrail on the pedestrian side, faced the sun, stretched out its wings so the white stripe shone on the underside, ten feet wide and trembling, the bird transformed into the image of the cross at the moment of first light. Whose meaning and weight both him and Harvell carried with them in their hearts from Pope County to that very spot, that intersection of the old world and the new at the John D. Lee Bridge, built and conceived as a monument to the man.

Birdy stood their trembling, the stripe white as fire.

Blow the son of a bitch. Push it.

The reasons they walked away from it were sealed in that moment, each of the named sticks of TNT screaming for vengeance, to take back what was taken from them on that bitterweed field of death. Or maybe not. What could the living do to harm the dead? Not let them die. And that's what they'd kept doing, wasn't it? Not let them die.

The percussive *whump* arrives as both surprise and a moment Edgar's felt coming for most of his life. He'd felt it back in Scranton when he'd tripped on a high hurdle, and again on the day preacher'd held him under so he could see the faces of his mama and daddy, brother and sister as they sang out *hallelujah, thine the glory,* and Edgar'd fought up for a breath new as a just born baby, and the sun in his eyes was forever. It had chased him when the black Peterbilt had run him off that Oklahoma highway, and again in the lightning hot teepee of the Coconino Detention Facility when Chief Joseph had slapped the side of his head with an eagle feather and said *be free.* Had it not been with him, the first of the Unknowns, when he'd first seen Rose Marie Yazzie in the mist of dream after Stoner'd hit him with the billystick?

When they lay together in a field of stars.

How long could spirits wait?

21.

According to Daddy's Aunt Ginger, who Luce had met that time she'd run away from home with Jackson Tripp—whatever in the world had become of Jackson Tripp?—and they'd thrown that fiesta for them with Uncle Davey where she'd maybe eaten dog, there was a history of women from far-off states being tricked into moving to Arizona, just like Grandma Josephine had been from Arkansas, on the run, married to Buddy Washer by a sleepy justice somewhere in the heart of Texas. She's getting ahead of herself, Luce. Daddy's story. Mom's. Hers now. Because, if it's true about the women being tricked and birthing children and the children birthing more children out there in the sagebrush desert, there'd be a whole tribe of them by now, maybe, spread from Tucson north and south to who knows where. Pumping gas and painting barns, tying steel in slabs and roofing houses overlooking mesas where the skeletons of Apache warriors caught in General Crook's crossfires lay mingled with the ones that came before and after and after that. There was no daylight savings time here, they'd set themselves in a bubble of time aside from the rest of the country. The great archipelago of Flagstaff like a sea island so you could drive through five habitat zones in thirty minutes, fly down into the Antelope Hills, First, Second and Third Mesas to Tsegi, Marsh Pass, a half hour drive from where she'd spent the night in

Dinnehotso, broken bread with Indians and Edgar who she'd driven over the spine of the continent because daddy felt indebted to the man for saving his finger that time when a man had bit off and swallowed it. The Martin was payback. She'd got it here, Luce. Only he'd run off chasing those two kids who'd been up to no good, blown something up out back and hightailed it, whose car Luce now followed at a distance, a junker blowing purple smoke. Just up there, she's keeping them in sight.

The thing to her right is Comb Ridge, three hundred feet tall, bald as an elephant's back. Eighty miles long, it ran down from Utah, some kind of upwarp from fifty million years ago or something. They'd hiked it along Butler Wash when she was four and the winter Olympics came to Salt Lake just after 9-11, and Daddy half expected a jet airplane to crash into the stadium just up from their house, so instead of attending the downhill or watching speed skating, they'd lived in Bluff at Recapture Lodge, went out on hiking expeditions every day then soaked in the hot tub and had happy hour in the afternoons, cooked dinner in the kitchen unit. The world had seemed magical then, when she was four, what she can remember of it. How they'd head out when the sun came up, Moondog, their long-dead Lab in the cold seat beside her, off on some bumpy road with the smell of coffee laced with Bailey's, and they'd dodge potholes all down Butler Wash along Comb Ridge until Daddy found the trail he was looking for. Steam rose from Moon's pee, the water bottles clicking against each other in her Raggedy Ann backpack. Mom with that look she got sometimes. And they'd turn a corner and there'd be a little village with an irrigation system and painted kiva, pottery and points and hands blown on stone walls. A thousand years old, Daddy said. People had lived there a thousand years ago. A great horned owl flapped up out of a juniper one morning, and Daddy'd lit sage, said it was a messenger between worlds, that it carried words from the dead to the living.

A wind came up and it rained, and the rain turned to snow before they made it back to the truck. What had they said, she wanted to ask, the dead to the living?

A sign says Marsh Pass, EL 6740. There's a burned down trading post where the boys turn, the jalopy blowing smoke past a sign with TSEGI in bright white letters. The road looks rough for street tires, even four new ones.

Dust rises against the blue sky. She follows.

Why not?

What would they be like, her Washer cousins? Would they recognize her as a relation? The whole thing about growing up with only a mom and dad, fifteen hundred miles and the Rocky Mountains between you and any other blood kin save the ones in Arizona who were taboo and not to be trifled with, about growing up gentile among Mormons, always on the outside with no windows to see through, you were always on the lookout for somebody, anybody, who could know you from the inside out, if that was even possible. Why hadn't they given her a sister or a brother? A twin. She's imagined it forever, someone to share secrets with, have a conversation without ever having to say a word. Have a pet name for. Go on diets with. Learn to drive. Fail math. Share grief. And maybe drive cross country on this wild goose chase for a stranger Daddy'd known in another state, another time and place. And now this. Following two kids down a dirt road for no reason in particular. On street tires. He'd have a cow, wouldn't he?

The rain had turned to snow and then to rain that never hit the ground. You could see it up ahead, sheets of it shining, only it never made it down. *Virga.* The messenger bird up there circling, able to see a rabbit at a mile, eyeing them, bearing the message she needed to hear.

Maybe it was for her, this wandering?

They didn't go far.

She's on them before she thinks to stop, the boys. The

blue-eyed one's face in the rearview, the Indian kid's hand out the window, palm up. A cloud of dust between them. The purple smoke.

The seat warmer's on, nice against her back.

9:57. 56 degrees, the Sube says. 3rd of May. Face-to-face graduation tomorrow at the University of Utah in Salt Lake City, where she was born under the full Wolf Moon on a January morning when corn snow fell, and an old man fed hunks of stale bread to pigeons at the fountain outside the hospital whose main floor was decorated with photographs of nuns, fifty of them in full regalia. The story of her birth, how and why it comes to her this second, parked not a stone's throw from the cave's dark mouth, she sees it now, up there yawning, for some reason the X that marks the spot that has brought them here.

Mom had gone toxemic.

They'd induced. Forty hours it went on daylight to dark and daylight to dark. He'd played jazz for her. In the maternity ward room that was decorated so that all the Victorian looking furniture transformed into some apparatus for birth. She's seen the room, Luce. He'd taken her there for birthdays some years, just walked right in—the center of her universe, he called it.

She'd wanted to do it without any drugs, Mom. So much for that. After the anesthesiologist administered the epidural, she'd finally begun to dilate, into the thirty-fifth hour now, January 15, 1998.

The OBGYN was also a trained midwife, so cesarean was out of the question. The drugs kicked in, and mom was brave. He'd said that—she was the bravest person he'd ever seen. One AM, he'd held her hand and together they counted: one two, three, four, five, and she'd push, and they'd do it again. Time went holy. He swears. A quarter size circle of her head shone through, more. And she was born at 2:32 a.m., her map of the universe radiating from there.

"She's a feisty one," the doc-midwife said, the first words ever spoken over her, because she'd screamed first thing, bawled, furious and alive.

He'd held her, rocked her and hummed a tune that he could only remember as the sweet sad music of humanity, and the woman who'd just delivered her said that it was something, his humming. Usually, they were watching a rerun of Gomer Pyle, she said.

He'd carried her down the hall for blood to be taken, and when they poked her heel, she'd screamed, and it hurt him to the core, that scream. Hadn't she heard it a dozen times, early in the Januaries of her life. *Guess what was happening today twenty years ago*, he'd say. Or *have I ever told you about the time*.

Yes, he had. And she'd remembered.

"You followed us," the Indian boy said.

He twirled his wrist for her to roll down the window, which she did. He wore a cowboy shirt with blue snaps. One of his front teeth missed a corner, and his smile was goofy and real.

"Why'd you follow us?"

And just when she was thinking of an answer to the smiling boy's question, another car pulled in behind them, a wave of dry dusty air rolling over them. Rita Begay, from supper last night. Edgar and Rose in the front seat with her. Here they all were. And if Luce had known the right way to look, east and a little south from Marsh Pass, she'd have seen Canyon de Chelly rise a hundred miles off in the desert, Mummy Cave and Antelope House, Tsegi Overlook, where someone with good eyes and a sense of direction could see them there that second.

22.

She'd thought to burn the letter, Roger's, the one where he was so, so sorry up one side and down the other, but when it came right down to it she didn't have enough of whatever was the opposite of love to even bother. One of his words, *bother*. Did you *bother* to do this or that or the other? A cruel word. It lay right now in a basket on top of the microwave, folded inside a *National Geographic* whose foldout was of gladiators, all the different kinds with their swords and armor and blood. Criminals were sent to gladiator school in the Roman Empire Days, where they went through boot camp, beefed up and learned how to fight with short not too sharp swords, because it was all about putting on a show. Some fought wild animals on the coliseum floor, lions and tigers, wild hogs. There were women gladiators who tussled with curved swords, bronze breast plates glittering with precious stones. There was this one kind called a Retiarius who fought armorless save a shoulder guard, trapping his opponents with a weighted net, then stabbing them with a trident. Sometimes he fought two at a time off a platform where there were rocks for throwing, fifty-thousand Roman rednecks in the stands hollering for the kill, the way they did at Dino Rodeo Days Fairground, when they turned a bull loose with three clowns before the finals of the bareback bronc competition. If Roger was a gladiator, that's what he'd be, Retiarius, trapping you with his net, then letting you have it. A photograph from *Musee Departemental Arles* shows these wind chimes where a gladiator does battle with his own penis, transformed into a wild boar or something. Imagine that, sword fighting your own dick. If she ever did write Roger back, she'd include this photo—say *don't bother to think of me when the wind blows*, or something like that. What he gets, isn't it? Netting her like that, sticking it to her. Temple-shrimple, the sword they'd made her swear on. She's done with all that, Joanna, they can all go back where they came from.

Lately she's been thinking of robbing the bank.

I mean, who better than a teller, she tells herself.

Back at the U in the pre-Roger day she'd taken Novel Writing Workshop with a heavy-set guy named James Odell who'd been a teller at University Credit Union, and his novel was all about a big robbery, perpetrated by a junior teller and his wife, who lived in University Village, just like James and his wife did. They'd all had to interview for the class, maybe forty some, and the cracked professor had selected him for that very reason, James claimed, because he'd once been a metal worker and now worked at a bank, and would be the best candidate possible for a bank robbery book. And he got it all right, seemed like. Side-stepping the vault alarm, the electronic angle, cameras, and the hardest part was dealing with the cash once the thing was done. What to do with it. How to avoid the trace. And the truth was that everyone got caught sooner or later. The professor said out loud in front of the workshop circle that he'd been teaching thirty years, and you could rob a bank and not get that much time.

Thirty years.

Maybe Roger could help her with a jail break. That was his business, jails. Lock down. Bread and water. He'd threatened to lock her up once, he really did. When she'd finally decided she'd had enough and started packing right in front of him. He'd said that there were ways to keep her around, make sure she didn't go anywhere. Always the holstered pistol and hand-cuffs to contend with, heavy enough to dent the dresser where he lay them at night. The little heart-side badge holes in his blue shirts. She could have stayed but for that last fight. It went too far. It did.

A masked teller at First Credit, the little rubber finger gloves on her right thumb and index, twenties, fifties, hundreds, would you like a copy of your receipt? Please sign here, point to the line and electronic pen, you can use your finger if you like. Would that be small or large bills? a camera in either corner, smile, excuse me sir, you'll need to take off those sunglasses, please remove the hood, what can I do for you today? I hope you have a very good one. Yes, it is cool in here, must be a hundred outside. We no longer require clients to wear the mask. Yes ma'm, crisp new fifties. Presents. I'll take whoever's next.

If she robbed the bank she'd run as far away from Vernal, Utah, as humanly possible, drive to Salt Lake International and take the direct flight to Paris, open, with no quarantine for fully vaccinated passengers, free liquor on the transcontinental, they could pour her into Charles de Gaulle. She'd do the exchange, rent a Yugo and drive south. Disappear and never come back. Make the getaway.

Her ship had come in. And then it had left.

That much is clear.

Everyone gets caught sooner or later.

Marrying a man, to *plight one's troth*. One page over from *trousers* in *The New Shorter Oxford, The New Authority on the English Language*. Troth. Middle English, a variation of truth. One's faith as pledged or plighted in a solemn agreement or undertaking. One's plighted word. A covenant. Troth-plight: the act of pledging one's word, especially in marriage. And there, just above, trousers and then *trounce*. Trouble. Troubled. Troublous.

Thursdays were the worst. The lull before everybody and

their mother rains in to cash Friday's paycheck from the Blue Diamond Mine, or Stratford or Peabody, the gas and oil leases from here to Timbuktu. And if you're teller on call, you have to stand there in your black mask, pretending that the last five minutes and the five in front of you didn't represent the far reaches of eternity, *and at my feet I always hear time's winged chariot*, and all that stuff.

Maybe she could write a poem about a bank robbery? What to rhyme with get-away?

She made quite the fashion statement
In her get-away
The velveteen leotard atuned as any garment
I do say.

Of course she'll lose her mind if she has to do this for another day, another hour, another fricking minute. The twenty-minute break juniors get every other hour on the hour too far off and she has to pee, she can feel it, a blue ache.

Roger'd had to wear a catheter for a week one time because of his prostate thing. A little brown tube that hooked to a see-through bag velcroed around his thigh on one end, into the dark eye of his penis on the other. It had to be washed with warm water and vinegar every morning, wiped with rubbing alcohol, along with the eye of his penis, and length of scrotum. Her job, she'd washed and cleaned for him, and it hurt like hell, she was sure of that. Woke him at midnight to take his medicine, and he'd needed her, counted on her, said she was saving his ass, and she was. And he'd reference that week in the letter on top of the microwave folded inside the *National Geo* with its gladiators with swords and armor. *I'm so sorry*, he'd said. *Please forgive me. We pledged our truth.*

For a comical second she remembers the hokey sword on its stand in the room of betrothal. How they'd sworn on it together, and she'd laughed because it was all just so silly, wasn't it? His brother the bishop saying the words. And then the business with secret names, to which she was not privy, nor ever could be until the world and all history ended and she got summoned to planet Roger with who knows who else, and they'd be happy for all eternity sealed as husband and wife, not even a *to death do us part to look forward to, so help me God.*

She'd gone through with it, Joanna. Given her word. And tried. Tried, tried, tried. But the last thing was too much. Wasn't it?

A camera up there in the corner catches her every move. Could it see her eyes and know the thought behind them? How she felt it that second on a Thursday forever afternoon in Vernal, Utah? Main Street out there with its flower baskets gushing in every storefront from here to Dino Museum where children were that second having photographs made with Barney and Bronto and Little Stevie Steg. Mom said she was feeling sorry for herself. Maybe so.

And maybe that's what was going down with Roger, too, feeling sorry for himself. And was love just when you directed that self-pity toward somebody else? Did she have pity on Roger? Did he pity her? Was it more than that, love? That's what she needed to study, everyone did, because when it came right down to it, wasn't that the one thing that had come about across the ages that mattered? Wasn't it? And she *had* loved Roger, she was sure of it. And maybe she still did, that's what this was about.

But the last thing. Could she love one capable of that?

Plight her troth.

Forgive?

23.

They'd buried her birth sack under a huckleberry in the school-yard. It would be the center of her universe, Rose's, and she'd one day come back to her people and teach the children what they'd taught her up north. She sometimes thinks of it down there, part Mama, part her, how the tree roots had entwined them and breathed their combined elements into bough and limb, where berries turned purple and stained the teeth and lips of tomboys until they vomited. Lord help her and Edgar if this baby ever knew. About the tree, the dynamite, grave digging and Big Cave One, what they'd found there, why. A great mystery, just like the rest. Imagine Granny Rose holding it up under the full harvest moon, throwing shadow wings, the veined intricacy of her mother's womb, dripping, translucent, a doorway home.

There would have been bone, eagle feather, fanned cedar, swaths of red cloth, white, yellow and black, a hank of horse hair from the fallow mare, corn, pollen. First frost about to fall. Words sung between worlds as that part of her raiment now shed to dirt, and even it shines beneath moon and star-eyed hunter, whose bow sends an arrow through the bull's red eye said to be the sky door.

How her digging stick had rattled stones, covering the mass on a bed of juniper, fragrant, medicine in it still, for a brave heart when need be. Huckleberry had bloomed like crazy at the end of each school year and the children's faces were smeared purple with pungent juice, their mouths and fingers. And she *had* come back, hadn't she? Class of 2014, they'd photographed her standing on a sandstone butte, the monuments behind her, Mitten Butte, others with the old names, a thousand miles of blue sky. Wearing the wealth of her household on each wrist, around her neck, the silver and turquoise, porcupine quill and arrowroot. Home to Dinnehotso. For a while, anyway, she'd come home.

When she was a girl, her father'd come home with a pay-check on Friday afternoon, and they'd drive over from the oil fields of Aneth and not get there till midnight. He'd always stop, Pops, on a bridge above the San Juan, turn the headlights on bright so they shone on the state line sign across the river, and the whole carload of them would get out and race to Arizona. Splashed in headlights, that's how they'd get there, running. Maybe he went on running and never came home. Into the lands of the woolly-headed Washers.

It was a saying, something Big Rose came up with, she was always telling tall ones. Like why they went up the dugway to Cedar Mesa at summer's end, set camp high where the pinyons grew, and picked for a solid week. Always go for the dark ones she'd scold, what's already fallen. On her knees in the good shade, gathering pinyon nuts with the smell of fire close to the ground, and nothing burns like that wood, orange and blue, cackling. Don't shake the tree, she'd say. You must not.

Why?

It would bring on winter, she said, flash her earth eyes as if everyone knew. Next thing you know you'll bring home a woolly-headed Washer, shaking the tree like that.

What's that?

What's what.

A woolly-headed Washer?

Flashed eyes again. The wild people, a whole tribe of them. They come from the South, don't you know, we all come from the south. She'd point with her elbow, half a bowlful already, the dark ones, more heart inside. Bear Ears over there, Mule Ear that way, rolling Comb Ridge blockading the river, at the end of summer so the chill came at night, early in the morning, and grandmother'd set the cast-iron skillet on coals, pitch in fistfuls of washed clean nuts. Let them roast. Pinch in salt. A little hissing, and that smell.

In the morning before light, that's when it was best. A blanket under pinyon trees with the orange and blue fire tongues, where the salted hearts hissed and were raw no more. In her own body. The place of her birth. The matrilineal line of her blood kin veined and intricate, shining beneath the great sky door. Between Star Man and Blood Bull. Where pinyon nut roasts on orange blue fire. That time, that space.

Edgar'd been a complete surprise.

Hadn't seen him coming.

Out there under the bridge that morning before New Year's, light on the Vermillion Cliffs and Mama sitting there with the pistol between her legs. Kuya, she called it, talked to it like it was a dog. Let's go for a walk, Kuya. You like biscuits? Good Kuya. Quiet that way it gets at Solstice, not a sound in the world save wind whistling over bridge spangle. And she'd walked out under the gun-blue sky, ice down at river level, lodged in an eddy, Paria Riffle up river, Marble Canyon below. Off for the holidays, there were cakes at home, half a sheep Lynyrd had braised over charcoal. Their little Christmas tree with its foil angel. The virus near out of control by then, they'd shut down the Nation, all the monuments. People were dying.

A world ago.

How Mama's driving them to the stash, where they'd buried it because Big Rose said no one would ever go there. Ghosts ruled the roost. No one would find it there. BC[1] they called it. Where this archaeologist had dug up a two-thousand-year-old teenage girl and her baby, carted them off to a museum in Massachusetts or somewhere. And the girl had something around her neck, a full scalp, skin from a whole head with the hair bobbed pretty like the Kachinas down on Second Mesa for the footrace. People were afraid of the place, no Diné would ever walk there.

She'd seen him on the far side, a movement against the abutment. Was that what it was called, abutment? She'll have to look it up, put Lynyrd on it. He was doing something, that man out there, to the rock. And it was cold out, first thing in the morning. Rose walked over, close enough to see the reddish shade of his hair, the rope tied around his waist, prying something from the stone every foot or so with a crowbar. Number Four condor under a spangle, black eyes glittering.

She said, "Hello?"

His crowbar skittered down the talus slope to a beam of shade, stopped. The condor flapped off the pedestrian bridge to its downriver twin. Wide-eyed Edgar, looked at her like she was a ghost.

"You scared me," he said.

Mom knew something about him, what he was up to. That there was some kind of trouble. She leaned over the rail so her hair fell down. And there he was Edgar Paris. Looking at her like she was a ghost.

"I'm sorry. Whatcha doing?"

He wore Levis, the rope looped through his belt, the cowboy kind, probably with his name tooled on it. The coffee was working on her, a thermos of it, up on Mom's table.

He said, "Nothing."

Smiled a little, a different kind of voice, she'd heard it in a movie once upon a time. "Get you a cup of coffee?"

He said, "Okay."

When she got back, he'd climbed up the bank, hidden his tools and untied the rope. The Rest Center was over there, picnic tables for tourists come to walk one side to the other and back. The concrete was cold, frost just melted. The kind of morning with a smell to it, make your breath come out in feathers.

He drank the coffee, chewed on the handful of pinyon nuts she'd sifted into his hand. With her eagle eyes Mom could see them from the other side. Now what on earth was Rose up to?

"Your name's not Washer is it?"

Edgar said no, his name was *Paris. Edgar.*

"Paris Edgar?"

"Other way around," he said. "You?"

She told him, and he said that he knew her somehow. From someone named Sister Begay, who she guessed was Mom, and that he'd seen her once there at that very place when he'd taken a blow to the head and she'd flown him on the back of that bird, a mutant angel, he called it, to a place up high and protected.

She said, "How about that."

"You had on turquoise, a silver belt."

The Class of 2014 photograph Lynyrd had taken, standing on a sandstone fin with the monuments in the background, that's how she'd been dressed, exactly. In turquoise and silver, new-tanned moccasins with white-woven leggings. Mom had showed him the picture.

"They eat dead skunks. Why would I choose to save you on a skunk eater?"

He thought that was funny. Skunk eater. They ate the pinyon nuts and sipped coffee, and before she knew it she was helping him load by moonlight, driving over Black Mesa to Dinnehotso and it was New Year's Eve. How she'd had him stop on the river bridge with the headlights on bright, and they'd raced across, laughing big frosty breaths.

How she'd got into all this, Rose Marie Begay. And now

the cave again, to disinter the grave they'd dug for it, where no one would ever walk, but did.

She'd missed one moon, then another. Maybe it was bad luck to go in there now. She needed a soda cracker. Warm ginger ale. The only remedy.

Stoner'd been back there, at the house. He was the man who hit Edgar in the head that day he'd dreamed her as an Indian princess come to fly him to safe haven. He was from Arkansas. DMF 936, his plates said, tags expired, the Natural State. I ain't no dumb mother fucker, he told her that New Year's Eve they met, the funniest thing.

Behind them, Valley of the Gods puts on a show, the sun just now shining on the Seven Sailors. She'd promised to take him there one day, Rose had. Into the lands of the woolly-headed Washers.

24.

South to Phoenix and north to St. George, Mama Linda's people could be trusted to backstab, dirty deal and deceive for small potatoes—the river permit scam, and the insurance finagle with that Tennessee Walking Horse named Yankee. They could manage the easy money. Two Dog, the Washer kid's dad, knew somebody in Tucson, and that person knew somebody in Nogales who knew somebody somewhere else that was maybe interested. He was a Washer, and Mama didn't trust him for two seconds, but he'd come through on the horse, had been his idea to begin with, buying the big red son of a bitch and insuring him to high heaven. Seventeen hands high, they didn't give horse flesh like that away, and she'd put up the jack, Mama had. Had the policy drawn up in her name for 25 K, though she'd tried for 50, no go. And when the horse up and died, she cut him a quarter, though he'd bitched and moaned for a third, threatened to tell, Two Dog had. And she'd given in, but not before showing him the knife. Cut his ass down to one dog. So anything had to do with a Washer was risky as hell, but what the hay. Truth was she was sitting on a gold mine and knew it. Maybe enough to get out of Dodge, if she played it right, which wouldn't be easy.

Now that they knew it was live.

Stupid as sacksful of hammers, those boys. Letting Stoney get wind of them, and he had it out for birdy to begin with, had sent him to the pokey once already for that business at the bridge, peeing on Granddaddy Lee. What was he thinking, Bird? They'd wired the bridge to blow, then lost their balls and walked away. Then, duh, couldn't just walk away from a hundred twenty sticks of primo Vote for Pedro. Somebody could get their head blown off—kiddos or German tourists, maybe take out one of the river rat flotillas all the time party-barging below. No, he had to *unwire* the bridge, Bird-man. And then Big Rose goes and talks them into burying the stuff in BC[1] because nobody'd ever go there in a million years, only they did.

Yazzie and the Washer kid. They'd dug some up, taking a break from spray-painting swastikas and smoking hooter. And *Drummer Hoff Fired It Off*, that was the long and short of it.

And now the business end. Two Dog knew somebody, though you couldn't trust him far as you could spit. The woolly-headed bastard.

He'd killed the horse, sure. You couldn't take that away from him. Injected oxygen into the artery, and that couldn't be traced, could it. His idea, even. And the dough'd come through, and she'd given him his part, and he'd complained. Threatened to tell. She'd shown him a lock-blade skinner. Put the fear of God in him. Or had she?

No matter. Business was business. He knew somebody. And that somebody knew somebody.

Enough.

She's just settled the matter in her head when two things happen that will no doubt kick the shit out of her ant pile. A decent morning with good light and smell of coffee, Lynyrd's. Good to spend the night away from that trailer with its history oozing out the electric sockets. And boy could that Big Rose cook, lay it on, which was something when you lived mostly on beans and potatoes, a Slim Jim from down the road if she was lucky. Rosey'd laid out backstrap and gravy, frybread hot from the skillet, a hunk of real cheese and not that that kind comes in a box, peach cobbler and ice cream, vanilla, Mama's fave.

The first thing was the house shook, and right after that the sound. Next thing, before she can say kiss my ass or how high's the water, Papa, comes a knock on the screen door where stands that stone man cop whose had it out for her since you know when. Later, she'd remember the dogs were barking, Thelma and Louise, she got them mixed up, they'd been really barking a lot. Cop at the door with a gun on his hip, already had the dirt on her, and then her stupid beyond belief offspring and idiot friend fired it off right under his nose? What she needed was a good long walk. Out the back door and down the wash, hit Laguna creek bed where the tall willows grew, keep her head down to the bridge and make for her place.

And that's just what she does.

Only he sees her climb out from under the bridge, Stoner. Flips his bubble gum machine on, let's the siren wail the one time.

Her trailer just down the dirt track on the other side. She could run, Mama could. And he could shoot her with that deer rifle he keeps behind the seat, her back big as a barn in the 3 x 9 scope. She'd never see it coming.

Blue lights with Comb Ridge behind them, the one wail. Easing toward her.

She walks like someone whose done nothing wrong walks, how she thinks they would. Take a stroll, whistle, maybe. Just out for a walk, Mr. Johnny Law. Long time, no see.

She must look a mess. Missed out on coffee. Bedhead. It's not fair. What's she done wrong? Who did he think he was? She owned the dirt she walked on, had buried a loved one in it. Mess with my morning walk, we'll just see about that.

Beside her now, the power window thrums down.

"Morning, Mama. What you up to?"

Dust on her tongue. From here she can see the effing dent

in her front door, tires rooftop to hold it down. She could hit it with a rock from where he'd stopped her.

The smell of him comes out the window, turns her stomach.

"Morning walk," she says. "I haven't been far."

Stoner nods. He says, "I see."

His radio chatters. There's a shotgun in a black rack, twelve guage, loaded with number one buck, maybe. The driver's side door has a white C on it, so if Linda stood back she'd see it was the first letter of *Coconino*, followed by *County* and *Police*.

She should walk.

The rock's throw up those steps, the silly dented front door that didn't even lock, who needed a key? Yazz's bedroom with its posters of black men, Daryl Dawkins, the go-rilla dunk. Dr. J. Kobe. Too bad about Kobe. Michael. LeBron. Maybe he hadn't seen her back at Rose's. Maybe.

She hadn't always been crooked, Linda. With just a few shakes of good luck she'd have been every bit as good as Rose Begay with her snooty college degree and Miss Native American University of Utah costume. They'd had to ride the bus to school up in Blanding, an hour one way and an hour the other. And if she wasn't top of her class, she was close for an Indian, and a girl. A reader, there'd been one teacher who could see what she was made of, Miss Crandall, who'd talked her into converting, being baptized in the name of Jesus and Joseph Smith. She'd read the book through, the one with the golden angel blowing a horn on its cover. She had a future, Linda Watchtower, as did all the Lamanites who converted. They could attend Seminary, have a doughnut for breakfast. All back before Yazzie was a thought, or even a possibility. Before his poetry writing father swept her off her feet with his silver tongue devil come on and the world transformed into a whirlwind tornado carnival ride for a while. For a while it had. And then he got hauled off to one big house or the other, more than one, and she grew big with Yazz, and all the gawky big-mouthed grandmothers had got wind of it and said I told you so, it's no Watchtower ever amounts to anything, is it? After, they'd hired her over to Navajo Parks and Rec at Window Rock, and all that had gone good for a while, hadn't it? Until one of the river rat parties had mistakenly mailed an envelope with four hundred and eighty dollars in cash for three days camping and hiking on the San Juan River, twelve dollars a pop per day per person. Who could blame Linda for figuring out what was what? She'd got caught and been fired. It was that simple. She'd moved on and raised her son and did best she could to get by.

It was that simple.

And now, Stoner.

"I really should be going," Linda said.

He nodded, Stone man.

And she thought she was home free, but of course she wasn't, never would be. There'd always be Two Dogs and Stoners and men like Yazzie's father, whose name she has erased from the book of her life, though it remained written on her heart as if carved there by a dull knife. In another world, she'd have converted and gone on a mission to Peru or somewhere. She'd have shed her skin and married, her sons and daughters would no longer be Watchtowers. Clean, she could live a good life. Couldn't she?

All she ever wanted.

25.

"Ever hear from Archie?" Stoner said, the name's long vowel rising to a question too dramatically so he almost regretted it, sticking it to her that way, not yet 9 AM, probably neither one of them had a sip of coffee. Glad to be shut of those dogs, the look in that one's eye. What did they feed the sons-of-a-bitches, make them mean like that? Back in his missionary days, they'd trained elders to sweet talk a dog, make it think it was his idea for you to give it a biscuit, hushpuppy. Those two unchained back at Big Rose Begay's, Indian dogs, hadn't had their shots, parvo, rabies, distemper. No telling what you get, one of those fuckers bites you.

Mama flinched. Bingo. She carried a knife, knew how to use it. Quartering chickens since she was a girl, skinning out antelope, winnowing sinew.

There was the boy to think of, a man now. Old enough to prosecute.

"That boy sure favors him."

You could only push an Indian so far before they shut you off. Went to their Indian place. He replays the scene: Arkie's truck, tags expired, easy money. A Subaru, Florida plates, ski rack—made no sense. Dogs on him out of the blue, one with the low moan, old glitter eye. Lynyrd, whose name was not Lynyrd, whistled, said something. Percussive *whump*. Not a gas explosion, enough horse in it to make the ground shake. Knock the front door, Arkie in his underwear. Rose, what on earth was she thinking, a girl like that, could have been somebody. Can I help you? I don't know, can you? She looked enough like her father to answer the Florida question, a Harvell, professor smart ass's daughter, no doubt. Mama Linda sneaking out the sliding glass, down to Laguna Creek, she knew what was what, didn't she. Big Rose with her chest puffed out, putting him in his place: *you here as a cop or a man?*

And that *had* put him in his place. What Joanna'd said to him, those exact words.

Rita'd turned the wrong way. She was supposed to be headed Lee's Ferry way, set up a table and sell mojos. She had the permit, everything was clean with Rita. He had no truck with her.

But she'd turned the wrong way.

Why?

Stoner felt himself on the cusp of a moment he'd been waiting for, and if he got it right, his life would fall back in place. And it all started with the woman standing outside his cruiser, looking at him like he'd just slapped her in the face, waiting for the next blow. Wednesday, hump day, he should have eaten.

"Tell you what, Linda."

She said, "What." Lifted her chin, gave him the look.

He said, "It's early. How about you get in. Let me take you for a cup of coffee."

Archie was Apache, matrilineal, believed in running their men off after they came of age, which he evidently had when he'd walked this way. Smooth, that long Geronimo ponytail. How was it the men tried to be prettier than the women, which was a task, likely, in Mama's case. She'd been a looker, word was. Something happened between them, moved into that trailer. It's not Stoner's fault, Archie's past.

"Some bacon and eggs. Hot cakes." He said it like he meant it, Stoner, and he guessed he did. He had nothing against Mama.

She was resourceful, and he admired that. He shouldn't have started out with the Archie barb, what was wrong with him sometimes? Sweet talk, the moment was at hand.

"On me," he said, unlocked the passenger door, front seat instead of the back, even though that was against code wasn't it, a total no-no. A violation that endangered vehicle and officer alike. Under no circumstances was the apprehended to be held anywhere enroute save the rear compartment with its steel mesh screen in between.

Too long in a hole, maybe he needed some human company? Was that asking too much? Hell with it. He met her eyes. Nodded. Motioned her to the door on the other side.

Strange how the women always wore tennis shoes. Keds, and a knee-length skirt, a yard of shawl wrapped around her neck. She'd thought to run. And what would he do if she did? Stoner?

Sooner or later they always ran. Even the non-guilty, made no difference, finally.

Out there somewhere, Joanna with the letter he'd put his heart into, asking her, begging her, to come home. The masked and unmasked, vaccinated and not, gentile and Saint, Lamanite, who God had turned from beauteous white to red for their sins. He'd never been any good at waiting, letting a moment play out as it would rather than forcing the hand. Story of his life, Stoner's.

But not today.

He waited.

Heard the raven *caw-caw-caw*, unseen but real, speaking to him from a place of reason, of consideration, of serenity and peace and forgiveness. *Caw-caw-caw*, the raven went, her sound, and if the Indian wasn't there staring knives into his face, he might have wept, how her voice went through him like a spear.

"Come on, Mama, I'm hungry."

A moment of human weakness, the dogs had sensed it, hadn't they. Sniffed it oozing out the pores of his skin, too long alone, holed up at Jacob Lake with no one save Elder Kavapulu and his dimwit wife to talk to, how the trailer stank of him, and he'd burned up all Joanna's letters so there was not one thing to save him from himself but now.

The waiting.

And if she ran, so be it. Let her go. Drive on home and get on with it. The holster digs into his right hip on the right side. A canister of bear spray, nasty stuff, why hadn't he thought of it, the bear spray?

She opens the door, her prints on it now. The seat swishes when she gets in, Linda Watchtower. She clasps her hands on her thighs, looks straight ahead, the trailer door Stoner once dented with the butt end of a scattergun. Archie inside hiding, her womany man.

Rolls the windows up, stone silence between them.

Turns around in Linda's dirt yard, heads east, 17.5 miles of wordless thought to the Monument and a place called The View, where there was a breakfast buffet and watery coffee. They drove in silence, the stone world splashed and big out there in the new sun. She smells of shampoo and frybread. Fear. Anger. What the dogs smelled on him. What he lacked. The road rolls out. He can see Utah from here, the way north to Joanna. All that name means.

The Valley of the Gods, they drive in silence.

Inside, the place was built like a kiva with windows instead of walls, so the first thing you noticed was the vast stone world spread out over a hundred and eighty degrees—Mitten Butte, Grey Whiskers, Rooster Rock, Mystery Valley. Luscious red rock rising from a sea of sage, juniper, stands of pinyon and rabbit bush. Wooden four-tops were set with flipped upside down water glasses and silver rolled in paper napkins, a carafe of ice water where they sat, a party of early birds or two with food cold on their plates. No beer nor wine, this is where they came for their honeymoon, Archie and Linda, wrote a hot check to the adjoining hotel, one of a chain south through Flag to Phoenix. Indian paintings decorate the window dividers, puny compared to the Navajo Nation, its panoramic arms thrown wide around them.

"So what's up?" Stoner said.

The buffet was eggs, potatoes, biscuits and gravy, under-cooked bacon, sausage, pancakes, three kinds of juice, coffee, weak, little French vanilla creamers. Silver rolled in paper napkins, little bands holding them tight. Tabasco. Ketchup. The lunch menu on the back side of breakfast, under plastic: half pound John Wayne Burger, Navajo Taco, try our famous Green Chili Stew. Sheep Camp Mutton, combining professional training with ancestral heritage.

Mitten Butte was just on fire out there, its one skinny finger flipped to the sky. The early birds have donned black masks, are giving Stoner and Rita the eye. Cop and an Indian woman at the hotel restaurant, her with bedhead and him wearing the pistol and cuffs, a canister of bear spray.

The biscuits are chewy, but the gravy's good, hard for even an Indian to mess that up. "Think of Yazzie," Stoner said.

Enough. You can only push a Indian so far.

26.

Someone with good eyes could gaze across the desert and see them there that second, where they've all been headed for the whole of their lives, only they couldn't know that, could they? Yazzie Watchtower, the blue-eyed Washer boy, Luce Harvell, and now, the dust from her car a swirl, Rita Begay with Edgar Paris and the pretty Rose girl—a raven tattooed on her shoulder. Here they all were, the heat from their motors ticking. Down a dirt road near Marsh Pass, Tsegi Canyon, a place with history. In the time of Christ, and before, a people now called Basket Makers lived and loved and died here, wove hundred-yard-long nets for rabbit drives and contrived intricate water systems with stone and gravity. They had religion, how they made sense of the world and cosmos beyond, what we all do, and it was all about rain, because rain was life and life was rain. The men grew their hair long and combed it into ornate styles, side bobs and shaved spots and the women had theirs singed off for rope making, the dark spot in the rabbit net that appeared to offer escape. They fired pottery, had brought the know-how up from Mexico which of course wasn't Mexico, all the research that said otherwise just so much bullshit. Her father was in history, he had the books. *Potsherds: An Introduction to the Study of Prehistoric Southwestern Ceramics; Basket Maker Caves of Northeastern Arizona; Handbook of North American Indians: Volume 9, Southwest.* As a girl, she'd grown up with them around, had lay in bed riveted by the black and white pictures of dog mummies and baby mummies, mummies of men and women and girls with their woven burial coverings sewn in two pieces with yucca, their faces shrunken to grimace. The chapters detailed the graves and everything found inside—digging sticks and cradles, skin sacks filled with corn and atlatls, beads and rocks and this kind of dice made of teeth for gambling. Game balls filled with ashes of the dead. They'd dug them up, these white anthropologists, and shipped them back east, where men with microscopes had a closer look. And though she didn't know it, Luce had stared at a page with the photographs of the very spot she'd come to now, Big Cave 1, where perhaps the most astounding find was recorded. A girl mama, with her baby, wearing a full-facial scalp tied around her neck, and what it meant, if anything, no one knew.

The guitar's back there, under the beach towel with mom's name stenciled on it, mewing a little when she hit bumps, all quiet now. He'd somehow lost a guitar way back when, and it, like everything else in Daddy's life, had a story. Something about the horse track at Hot Springs, and hitting the last race, a long shot, scoring enough moolah to buy the Ovation back from a girl who'd lent him money, only his girlfriend, who was ten years older than him, had too much beer to drive, so Dad was behind the wheel in race traffic. He'd rear-ended a guy, and the older girlfriend had demanded the longshot money to pay her deductible and that was that—he never saw the guitar again.

By the time he bought the Martin, he'd turned a corner. He had degrees, their marriage had held, she'd been born, Luce, and he taught a Saturday class, put all the pay toward the instrument made by hand that same year, 1998, in Nazareth, Pennsylvania. The layaway receipt's in the case, along with the original owner's card with *Joey Harvell* typed on it. Serial Number 642551, which proved the year, same as her. $1648.42 smackeroos, and worth every bit of twice that now, twenty-three years later. What had brought her here.

To this spot.

Why did you follow us here? the boy asked.

Probably she's been asking herself that same question since pointing the Sube north on A1A, the long, long haul from Georgia to Alabama, Mississippi up to Little Rock, and Solgahatchia on the authentic Trail of Tears. Oklahoma and Texas and New Mexico with her blowout, then four new tires and head gasket and the night on the lake and the tent with light glowing inside, sign for a two-headed snake, Land of Enchantment, Shiprock, Canyon de Chelly. Headed west. California out there. Not so much California as the dream of California, what it had come to stand for for the Okies and Arkies and Chinese and Japanese. A new beginning. A chance to start over. Hope. A there.

Wasn't that why anybody went anywhere, hope for something better?

Why they got out of the cars and stood in the dirt beneath blue sky, the cave mouth dark above them. North-facing, cold inside. Don't touch it with a ten-foot pole. Wednesday, May 3, a long day already. A good eye could see them from far away.

Why had she followed. Guess she'd find out.

Rita told her hello, summoned the boys so they all sat in a circle and began again on a conversation they seemed to have had before, only it had been interrupted, and now they had to finish. Luce was permitted to listen, she was part of this somehow now, if not before. Edgar sits cross-legged, Rose on a blanket beside him. The blue-eyed Washer boy and Yazz, whose mother, Linda, had been back at the house when the dynamite exploded. And that's what had happened, very much so, a stick of dynamite had gone off, though how it got there or why, that's what the talk's about, the speaking circle, Luce asked to say her part, to add it to the story. The circle.

She knew some of the threads that the talk circled back to, how the Mormons had walked down the canyon into Salt Lake Valley, and the travails they'd had that drove them there. How they'd planted corn on the day they arrived. Famine and grasshoppers and seagulls, all that. And already the land had been lived on since long before the Ice Age, when hunters had stalked giant sloth and camel, woolly mammoth and bison, how they'd walked to Tierra del Fuego at the tip end of what would be South America, and then walked back. The Spanish had come and run a slave trade, sought gold, *El Dorado*, found poor pueblos with their metates and pulque, tried to make them into Christians, but couldn't. Hopi and Diné, Paiute and Ute. Kit Carson and General Crook, a cast of characters bathed in violence and death, just as the Folsom and Clovis, who'd slaughtered the ancient mammals to extinction, then disappeared themselves. Basket Makers who'd flourished along the San Juan, whose medicine could be found at canyon mouths where granaries were stone-masoned into cliff clefts. Who'd built pit houses and painted kivas, whole human heads lodged in the air ducts for who knows why? They brought pottery firing skills from the south, net making, the old-time religion of flesh and blood, father sky and mother earth. For many thousands of years, more, this world was theirs. Around 1299, for reasons not entirely known, they walked away too, vanished.

Navajo filled the gap. Hopi. Others. 1492, Columbus sailed the ocean blue. More Spaniards. Florida. New Spain. Inquisition. Pilgrims. Wham bam. A whole lot of shaking going on. Fire and brimstone. Quetzalcoatl. Jesus. The sickness, came and came again. Two-hundred-year drought, followed by rains. The desert bloomed and went on blooming. Salt Lake, the ancient flyway, the Mormons had stumbled in in 1849, said *this is the place*, but of course that had been said before, and will be again. There's a name for the rage of the persecuted righteous. Rita couldn't remember it, but that's what they had, the Mormons. And they believed the apocalypse was at hand, and that they had a role in seeing that it happened in a good way. They were God's chosen people, just like the Clovis and the Folsom and the Basket Maker, Pueblo and Hopi and Diné before them, and how somebody else will believe after. The people of God.

And their prophet had been killed, the Mormons', by the people in a state that maybe touched the state where it happened. And these people in the state that touched the state, when they walked west, they'd had to travel the old trails, and had got caught in the rage felt by the persecuted righteous. Only this time the murderers had dressed up as Indians, they were certainly not the real deal, though it really didn't matter now, did it. The Arkies had been slaughtered, 120 of them, give or take. Left to the wolves, because that's what real Indians would do, right? Certainly, Christians'd never go in for such.

Story got out, published in a fancy east coast magazine with drawings of wolves eating little tow-headed girls. Big news for a while, then not. People forgot.

And some didn't.

Luce's father, and Edgar here, they'd sought revenge. Procured contraband and wired it to Navajo Bridge which had been named for John Doyle Lee Bridge before that, name of the one man executed for what had become known as Mountain Meadows Massacre.

But they'd lost their nerve. For whatever reason, Doc Harvell had walked away from the detonator. Edgar'd removed the explosives at great risk to life and limb, and had buried it here at BC^1 because Big Rose had had a dream that that was the right thing to do.

And so here they were.

Circled.

Rita talking, Grandfather Sun Bear, *Koyanisqatsi*, world out of balance. They should build a fire, she said. Do this right.

Here on this spot.

Sacred ground.

27.

Holds the tobacco to the sun and prays. Tunkasila, that he might do things in a good way. Know his heart, have pity. So the land might open itself to him, be his teacher. A fine day, early still, a wild donkey stud—stock from Coronado who raided mesas—brays in open delta where Chinle braids into river, Mule Ear diatreme just downstream, fossil throat of an extinct volcano. A wild land, this. What it must have been like to believe one's people to be the only ones on earth here, and then spot the ancient enemy on yonder anticline against the rose-pink world, lay stone in the clefts of cliff face, mason the seams tight, so corn from the millennium past is there for the grinding, masa, staff of life. The trail turns into shade just beneath the cliff, sixty feet, maybe, a little scree, how on earth did they climb there. Twenty steps north, in the lee of a corner where the patina is dark with mineral, Baseball Man, a golden eagle at his feet, Star Woman ripe with child. Chinle Creek not thirty feet away, cutting down the canyon's slight grade, bear tracks in the mud that morning in 1916 when Alfred Alfonzo Kidding found the mouth of the ancestral highway north, every major drainage home to the Clovis and Folsom hunter, who bequeathed to Basket Maker the ownership of earth and sky.

They lived here.

Right here.

Hard to walk without stepping on a shard, every flat

surface glyph-hammered, more alive in Four Corners a thousand years ago than today. From where Baseball Man gazes out the canyon mouth to the river, across the wash, trapezoid warriors with ducks for heads, remnants of the underworld guides who'd shown them forever. A spot that seems to pivot, Kidding looks up canyon, sees the cave openings with visible structures built into them, green from the springs that bubble from the sandstone whose aquifers hold the same sweet water those lips sipped in a time beyond time. Holy here in the desert, springs named Matrimony and Bridal, drink from them and you'll marry the water forever.

Sometimes the land will open itself to you. If your heart is right, sometimes it will.

Willows thrive along the creek bank where raccoons have left tracks, desert big horns and deer, raven. Six-feet across, the faintest sign of trail, he follows, climbs a blind bank that opens to a slick rock wash that holds water, a pool where tadpoles flutter, where time stands still and the earth opens its door and lets him walk in.

A pool with a ledge above it that makes shade. Frogs, tiny black tadpoles swimming in cool water. He goes to his knees, dips his face and drinks. It is good. Unlaces his boots, takes his shirt off, his pants, lets himself sink into the water so his head is under and he sees the sky through it. Clean, chill, Jesus bugs skittering. A delight to the flesh and blood, what makes him so different, Kidding, from the ones who came before? After? No before or after, only now. The air tanged with sage, cottonwood, willow. Birdsong. Wren? The days of his life slide away and he *is*. A song comes to him, his. One breath and then another. Amphibian. Relatives. *Metakuye Oyasin*. All my relations.

Crawls out onto the slick warm rock, lays on his back, the good sun there, breeze from up wash, sleep comes and when he wakes the world is quiet. Watching him, waiting to see.

A bed of clay, perfect for firing, the quartz content just right he sees straight away, deposited at the foot of the slick rock. It fans out before the creek beside the invisible trail. He smells it, the mud. Sun-dried, clean, breathing. Kidding knows that whatever has drawn him here is about to make itself known, and he wants to put the moment off, let it drag feet in coming. The eyes that watch him are not entirely unfriendly. They do not mean him harm. An hour has passed. Maybe two. The light is different. This is a good place, very good. The frogs and darting tadpoles, life, living. Bare feet on slick stone. Smell of mud. Wren. Raven. Caw-caw. Is it possible for a moment to never end? To go on happening inside of you forever? He's a man of science, but first a man, all that entails. The freight train of baggage back through space and time, cellular then multi-cellular, sea bacteria evolving to eye, and if you believe that, as the poet said, you can believe anything at all.

When he's an old man, Kidding, he'll have them bring him here when it's all said and done, the place that accepted him as himself, a space to dip one's face in the immortal waters beyond time, pledge one's troth to eternity.

Dressed, he climbs the bank to a plateau with a view of the far-off cliff cave in one direction, and the forever of canyon in the other. A yard of dirt and stone smaller than his backyard back in Cambridge where he'd buried black Moon under the plum tree wrapped in wild sage and owl's wings. He feels it here, the place opening to his consciousness. A slight grade to the bank, Chinle, a wall of umber sandstone on the upper side and a house rock with cavities. Kidding's glad he's by himself. Washed clean, maybe an hour's passed, maybe two, Baseball Man back there as watchman, Star Woman, cave in the distance. Green with poison ivy. He takes a breath. On the ground, embedded in rivulets and cryptobiotic folds, pottery shards, Mancos black on white, corrugated, the great invention that allowed more surface area to be heated, and therefore increased heat potential, the lips of pitchers, a handle, bone, buff colored point, a human tooth, all on the three-foot square above the house rock. He moves slowly, chooses where to step. Clouds are coming, sailing over, throwing shadows. On the lee side of the house rock, a boulder with a flat table surface. Hammer stone with both ends scarred from working chert. Pressure flakes in piles, three dark points and a milky quartz knife blade. He sits above the table rock, the seat perfect, with a back rest and all day shade from the house rock, sees the pottery kilns just over there, picks out glyphs on the umber face, a sunshield, flute player with phallus dangling, spiral flowering beneath a moki walkway that climbs past two writhing rattlesnakes. On the other side of Chinle, the humpbacked folds of buckled draws and sandstone, another cave with visible structure, and the way south, Indian road, Poncho House, Inscription House, Wolf Man Ruin, Rabbit Ears, painted kivas and ball fields and houses of the holy unforgotten dead. The hammer stone fits his hand perfectly, and the table rock, pocked and sturdy, is just the right height. Of course it is. More flakes than he's ever seen in one site, warm jasper, six varieties of chert, traces of obsidian and the unlikely quartzite with its signature compound from the Ouachita Mountains in Arkansas, run west in extinct rivers before there was a such thing as west. The cool shade and spirits watching, entirely in their fold.

A sense of peace, the world feels right. He belongs. To something bigger than himself. And Kidding both wants to hide this place and show it at the same time. How it gets in your blood. He could sit in this workshop forever, feels for the world like he's been here before, the light and cloud darkening. Maybe a streak of lightning to the south and west, low thunder, he smells rain before the first fat drops thwack the tablestone. Holy fall rain, it comes while he sits with his back to the stone at the work table, hammer stone in his right hand, working the chert, pressure flaking a tiny point, one for rabbit, another for sheep, one for gigging the whiskered river catfish and another for goose and heron, wild turkey gobbling sunrise. Hand knives and scrapers, the size one makes to kill a man, pierce lung and heart. One for buffalo, another for mammoth, should she ever return.

Donkeys bray from the river and the rain is holy, sudden then gone. And the sun comes out, the earth shakes itself off and is new again. Some mojo there. The cottonwoods golden, and the wash picks up, swishing. There's a woman back in Cambridge, his wife, her name is Jillice. A daughter by the same name. They've written him letters, no doubt, forwarded to Kayenta where he'll reprovision. Mail what he's collected back to the Peabody for cataloguing procedures, and all that comes with that—not his cup of tea. They'll be waiting for him when he steps from the train, the Jillices and he'll go home to the house on Montague Street where black Moon is buried in the backyard under a plum. When the 1916 tour of the Southwest is over and the entirety of the finds recorded and catalogued, and he's accounted to all who've funded the expedition, he'll rejoin that life. He will love and make Christmas cards with snippets of poetry, unrhymed. He'll shave in the morning and take his coffee black. The days and weeks and months will come. They surely will. But a part of Kidding will ever be seated with his back to stone and the workbench before him, the hammer stone perfect in his hand pressure flaking the stone age points with fat cold holy rain thwacking his face, his hands, his heart, his soul. With the eyes of the gods on him, entirely in their fold.

The last thing, he can't bear to take.

On the bank above the house rock, rain has exposed a delicate shard. Black triangle, flagged at each point on white ware, a pattern that replicates so the triangles pierce other triangles which become stars, and those stars part of larger stars. Infinity, he sees, between his thumb and index finger. Perfectly intricate, it is the finest piece Kidding's ever seen anywhere, and he feels heartfelt kinship with the maker, her skill and precision and nuance of hand. Her teacher. A vessel fit for ceremony, a wedding feast, the perpetuity of blood kinship across space and time. From the wet backpack, he digs out the Kodak, unsnaps it from the leather case and advances the celluloid film one snap. Kidding stages the piece in buff sand, just as he found it, the sun full on the thrice ticked triangles that make stars and those stars stars. Like the Anasazi spirals that unfurl forward and backward with equal movement, the piece is quite literally forever. Both linear and curved, the warm black triangles are both phallic and feminine, ethereal yet part and parcel of the material world. Infinity insinuated by a single point in curvo-linear time. Forever and not forever.

Kidding tucks the precious find beneath a fold of House rock, hesitates, desires it for himself, though he knows it's not his to take. None of it is, really, is it?

Small enough to fit in the palm of his daughter's hand, a portal to forever though not forever. Passed through fire and blood and song. Heaven and earth.

The same thing?

28.

What she needed was a soda cracker, Edgar figured, a can of warm ginger ale. They'd left without breakfast, out the back door and into the arroyo that skirted Laguna creek along Comb Ridge. Following the fool boys who'd somehow managed what Edgar and Harvell had not, to set off one of the UNKNOWNS in broad daylight, draw the cops like stink on shit. Yazzie and the Washer boy, they'd hightailed it, made for Louie's jalopy and drove toward the cache, where him and Rose'd buried it in the faint light of the big cave that overlooked Valley of the Gods. Now, Johnny Law was on them. Every piece of it traceable to him and Harvell, their prints—the whole nine yards. His truck back at the house, expired plates, Arkansas DMF 936, dumb mother fucker, that was him, Edgar. The whole nine yards of it, dumb, dumb, dumb. And now this. Take care of it the right way this time. What Rita Begay said. Rosie's mama, big Kuya under her skirt. It was still wired, the stuff. The detonator still intact. Edgar guesses its possible, but still illegal as hell. Not as bad as the other, though, taking out the bridge. He'd do it, he would. This very morning, why not? But Rose had left without breakfast, and the sickness was on her. She needed nourishing. The thought of the life inside of her, that it was part him, and therefore everyone he'd ever loved, almost, wobbles his knees.

"Anyone got anything to eat?" Edgar asks the circle, when Rita quits talking.

The Harvell girl has juice in the cooler, cheese and crackers, and a slice of leftover pizza, Italian sausage and mushrooms, black olives. Lemonade.

"Ugh," Rose says. "Crackers."

He follows her to the car, Luce Harvell. Inside a plastic bin with Blue Moon written on top, in the hatch of the Subaru beside a beach towel, lots of goodies, fancy crackers.

"Thanky," Edgar said. "You got ginger ale?"

"Mom's drink. She mixes it with bourbon."

"We don't want that," Edgar said. "Diet Coke?"

"I don't drink soda. OJ?"

"I guess," Edgar said. Truth was he was hungry too, as he ever had been, too many nights back in Pope County living off pinto beans and potatoes, ketchup sandwiches. "I'll take that slice of pizza if it's okay."

She looked like her daddy, the Harvell girl. Had his sweet streak as well, if not the temper. Above them, the cave mouth with a spray-painted Chicago Bull off on one side. Dollar signs that weren't here before.

The juice jug is cold, he'd like to take a slug straight from its mouth.

"I have something for you here, too," she said. "When it's a good time."

Edgar said, "Thank you," took the food and drink to Rose, who'd missed two moons and was feeling it. She turned the jug up, chewed a cracker, and nodded. Yes, better.

Yazz and Washer were in the junker, listening to gang music. Rita's in the Chevy, she'd picked them up, said, "Need a ride?"

"I don't want to go back in there," Rose said. "Not like this."

"How's 'at juice? Don't blame you."

Technically, today was a teaching day and Rose was under contract, but everybody and their mother had service out here somehow, and she'd called in sick, first time since Christmas break, when they'd met, and she'd raced him across the river bridge and all this had started. A long, long time ago, seems like, who could have guessed?

"What do we do?" He'd go up there and reconnect it all, stretch the wire far as he could, blow it. Make everybody get way back. Disappear the evidence.

"I'll go up there," Edgar said. "Take care of my end."

Rose took a bite of pizza, then another, stripped sausage chunks off and chewed. "How do people eat mushrooms," she said. "It doesn't sound safe."

"Probably not."

Off near the highway, a car crunched gravel. Mid-morning, what he'd give for black coffee, a sausage biscuit.

"You rather dig it up and sell it? Go to Hawaii with Linda?"

"We need to start thinking," Rose said. "Does she have more pizza?"

"How long do you think?"

She had a smile, Rose did. That goofy sideways way that made Edgar wish he'd known her when he was twenty years younger and people wouldn't look at them funny—at *him* funny—when they walked in somewhere together. When he was thirty some and the world was in front of him, before jail time and the bridge mess. They could have gone to California and lived by the seashore, afternoons sipping *sake* and watching grey whales blow their spouts.

"December," Rose said, that smile. "Christmas baby."

His mama'd kept a snow globe on the mantle of baby Jesus in the manger, Mary and Joseph and wise men on camels. The little baby was reaching his arms out, and when you wound it up the thing played *silent night, holy night, all is calm, all is quiet.* She'd had it a long time, the baby Jesus snow globe, and the water inside had turned yellow. But it was always out at Christmas, with MaMa's lavender smelling pie and the tin angel with candles, little bells dinging.

The car'd stopped, Edgar halfway registers, out there beyond the hill, the two boys rat-tat-tatting the dashboard to the gangster music, Rose hog-gobbling Original Wheat Thins with torn off hunks of Colby Jack between them.

"Guess I best get this done."

In the car, Rita was talking on her phone, nodding yes. The Harvell girl stood outside her open hatch like she was waiting for something. The two boys wild to be wreckage forever. What some poet had said, Joey Harvell always quoting.

Rose said, "Be careful" and "I love you."

And it was enough, plenty.

"Boys," Edgar said.

And for the second time in his life he entered the north facing cave, chill to the bone, and a smell you forgot until you remembered. If the thing could talk, what words were big enough to hold drumbeat and wailing, firelight on the green-striped face tied around her throat, dead young with child, it seeing through the fog wall of forever and ever. In what strange tongue would love be said, be careful, all is calm, all is quiet.

Inside, there was more light than before. Chill. The north facing door where scree had fallen, yellow sun shaft falling that second on the Harvell girl, "I'm part of this, too," she was saying. The boys wearing their dinky headlights that cast weary shine on a wall where white dots splashed every two feet or so, startled by the black demons, naked women, an intense Satan with curved horns, MANIFEST DESTINY and more dollar signs, spray painted on top of glyphs unmolested for two-thousand years. Cists with human rib bones visible. Lurid, they had not escaped whatever wild energy drove Yazz and Washer to do what they did, finding the goods only by accident of their graffiti spree. There was a smell, like the alligator den in Little Rock where Big Arkie slept in a concrete pool, pigeons pecking hell out of his back so you figured no way was he alive, and then the old son of a bitch'd come to life, snap jaws and bye-bye birdie. And the air had a stale taste about it, like it had been breathed too many times and had come here to rest. And over there, where they'd buried it. One hundred and eighteen sticks of contraband dynamite with the names of Arkansawyers slain at Mountain Meadows, north and west of Tsegi, not too far.

"For Daddy," Luce Harvell said, who'd been there all those years ago, before the plague or Rose Begay or ever having laid eyes on the Valley of the Gods or Big Cave One.

Viva Las Vegas, one wall said. Another, unspeakable.

On the way in, somebody'd burned down the trading post, and all the house trailers on the side of the road that overlooked the entrance to Tsegi Canyon. They'd passed through a gate that said NO TRESPASSING. TRESPASSERS PROSECUTED TO THE FULL EXTENT OF THE LAW. TURN AROUND AND GO HOME. JESUS SHAVES. Concrete stairs climbed to nothing, and on the backside of a wall was the same rendition of horned Satan as now decorated the way looking at the four of them that second, when the State Trooper cruiser crunched up behind the silver Subaru, died, and the doors opened, then shut.

Sounds too muffled for hearing by those inside, but all too clear for the one out there, Rita and little Rose.

The Watchtower woman.

Stoner.

The esteemed Harvard archeologist, Alfonzo Vance Kidding, sewn into a Zuni death shroud not unlike those he'd excavated from Big Caves One and Two, White Dog, Kimboko, and the other nameless ones, lay buried just on the rise, unmarked as he'd requested. Those whose cists had remained hidden, and the angry spirits of those found, who were said to dog the tracks of anyone desecrating by entrance, so you could feel them there, intent on harm between realms, their spirits manifest. And now that Yazzie Begay and Louis Washer had so stirred the shit with their spray-painted tits and asses and electric guitars splattered over the altar of the holy, the prayers said there, the old words, Tsegi Canyon and BC¹, once again rife for the moment at hand.

He reconnected the mainline, Edgar. Each of the 120 pieces was still wired to the whole. With a couple twists, the detonator's flickering piezo-electric tongue is live.

Of course, Mama Linda spilled the beans. Think about Yazzie, Stoner'd said, and she had. She had. The ten-inch skinner cold against her thigh. She'd thought of her son, and his father, about poetry and sunrise and the quiet place inside she'd known before all this.

What Rosey'd give for a soda cracker and warm ginger ale, the pizza hard on her tummy now, not the right thing, no, not at all.

Rita, with her sacksful of mojos. Kuya. The world out of balance.

The D-28, and thus Joey Harvell, mewing ever so slightly when Stoner slammed his door, so those in the cave could hear it, but not the words that followed. Everything wired now, ready to roll.

Little white letters circling the canister of bear spray on Stoner's right hip, what to do, what not to do.

Valley of the Gods just on fire with light, the blood red hues both a comfort and affliction to the unshielded eye.

29.

Once they acquire taste for the flesh and blood of their kind, chickens can be real assholes. You can try to break them of the cannibalism, you can try. After the dust settles and everybody's gone, Big Rose breaks out the Pick No More, Blu-Kote and Vetericyn, green latex gloves and the water hose, high pressure nozzle screwed on tight. She dons Lynyrd's rubber boots and a hairnet, talks to them through the silver wire like they can hear and understand her every word. Where everyone's off to is a mystery to Big Rose, whatever lights their candles. Lynyrd'd come skulking in when he's hungry, stash of frybread in foil on top of the microwave. Busted a whole basket of eggs this morning. In all her life, Big Rose had never heard of a single person dumbfuck enough to bust a whole basket of eggs.

"You know I could just break your neck right now. Get it over with."

The trick is to whomp them to the back of the coop with a broom, reach down and grab whoever you can. Carry them to the table for doctoring.

She'd let it go too far this time.

The three Rhode Island Reds' backs are bare and bleeding. Wing feathers picked to red meat on the worst one. The vents—what her University of Nebraska-Lincoln Poultry Management Guide calls *cloaca*—are a mess. Somebody's feeding on flock mates in the act of laying. Big Rose shakes the image from her head.

The Sex Links, now whittled down to four, have fared little better. They miss tailfeathers, the undersides raw red. Her third, fourth flock, the A-frame coop, stapled with chicken wire, was once Little Rose's play station with its swings and slides and gauzy pink fabric from Cortez fluttering during their princess games. When she'd wear a tiara and the jingle dress Grams made for her, point a willow wand at a dog or cloud, say *presto chango* in that silver-plated voice she'd got from the wind.

A lifetime ago, now.

And this. The cannibalism run amuck. She'd tried. Big Rose had. She'd done everything the manual said, and had the uppity white girl at the feed and seed explain it backwards and forwards.

Three times she'd doctored them now, the wounded.

And who's going to let you catch them without a chase? She ran them against the back fence, swiped up a Sex Link, carried it flapping to the table. A bucket of sudsy water was situated there with two rags—one to wash and one to wipe. It would be better if Lyno was here to hold them, but he's not, is he?

No sign of improvement whatsoever since last time. Worse, even. She'd found this one's twin under the coop lip with a hole pecked clean into the guts, a brown egg having rolled out of it there at the end.

Rose washed and wiped. Squirted antibiotic, then smeared on the foul-smelling Pick No More, which must taste ungodly. Finishes off with the Blu-Kote. Miss uppity white girl had told her she must be careful with the stain, showed her a store shelf where it had spilled twenty years ago and had not faded one iota. What she said, *iota*. Wear gloves. Well, duh.

And it must burn like hell, given how this one screams bloody murder. She throws her through the door past the water decanter someone's shit all over, chases down a barebacked red, hauls her to the table.

The chickens won't dare peck each other while Big Rose's looking. She'd camped out in a chair behind the pear tree trying to catch the culprit—no go. Could be anyone. The book says to provide foraging opportunities. Plenty of space. Try mash instead of pellets. Beak trimming as a last option. Hang white strings around the coop to divert the peckers. To remove victims and euthanize humanely.

Humanely?

What the book said.

How exactly do you do that?

Kill humanely?

It's what all this was coming to, Big Rose knew it, and so did Lynyrd who'd somehow managed to dump the whole egg basket this morning. Bad luck. Bad, bad, bad. Like the hen with a hole pecked into her gut dribbling out that last brown egg. Eating it was out of the question. For the second time Rose shakes the image from her head, her appetite all undone.

Nine chickens left of the dozen they'd panic bought that freezing spring morning when the virus had hit the Nation hard, people dying left and right, and she and Lynyrd'd driven to Cortez at 3:00 in the morning, sat in the truck with the rest of the scared shitless idling in the parking lot, no toilet paper in the stores, little meat, forget eggs. The load of chicks had arrived at sunrise, a black semi unloading into the backside of IFA, and they'd all had to take a number, stand masked in a line that stretched from the double glass door out across the lot. They stood there, Lynyrd and Rose, with the rest, some with kids or dogs, a few on walkers. And the sun rose up over the snow-clad San Juans, Sleeping Ute, Shiprock off over there. Her number'd been fourteen. Lynyrd was twelve. They went all the way to three hundred, somebody said, the numbers.

Sun rising on the mountains, turning them pink, the steam rising from their faces. It had been an act of hope, driving to Cortez for the chicks. Maybe the first hopeful thing in a long while. Her and Lynyrd standing in that line with the numbers in their hands.

They'd prepared a little place back at the house, a warming light and tin feeder, one of the dog's bowls for water. You were allowed six apiece, and Lynyrd'd gone with the Black Marans, because who knew? Rose had selected the Sex-Links and Reds, pretty birds that chirped and bawked in the floorboard all the way back to Dinnehotso, lived in the house, shared the space, the Hope Chickens.

And they'd laid up a storm, hadn't they?

Once they got started, they had. Ten, twelve a day, seventy so a week, they'd had eggs running out of their ears. Frittatas, omelets, fried and scrambled, over-easy, poached, homemade mayo, deviled, soft-boiled, whipped into breads and puddings and cobblers, they'd gone to town, must have cholesterol of ten-thousand or something by now. They'd traded them at the post for anything they wanted, T-Bone, even. Big Rose's eggs, laid by the Hope Chickens down on Laguna Creek.

You had to watch out for raccoons and hawks, little bastards. It was a brutal world out there if you ever forgot to close the coop. Walk out one morning and find one with its head chewed off. Nothing else, just the head.

A Sharp-shinned could snag one from the run in a heartbeat, rip its heart out beating in the cottonwood, glare at you with those beady eyes.

And you'd protect them, they were yours. You'd shoot the coon if you ever caught it, snare old hawk man, kick the dog if it even thought about funny business.

Get out of here.

The virus would peak and subside. Edgar'd come down with it, Little Rose. There'd be a stay at home order and quarantine with your pod, Stay Safe, Stay Put, Turn Around and Go Home. A medicine man'd come around with shots in springtime. It was all part of something bigger. She'd had the dream of herself grown young, out off Comb Ridge on Butler Wash having wandered up on the ruin and found the slick-worn green as grass shard on the kiva lip. And thought it was trash. That some violator had thrown it there as trash. Took it, and paid. How the great horned owl had burst up from the cedar and the spirits had chased her. Wind had come, blew grit in her mouth—the blown-out tire and scorpion sting. She tastes it this second. Sun Bear's prophecy, the world out of order.

She'd told them to bury it at BC[1]. She had. It had made strange sense, the named ones and the unnamed. Mother and child. Husband and wife. Son and daughter. To the lightless place that opened north, portal gate, where no green thing grew. A glimpse of God Valley. Time before time.

Where they were all headed now, what this was coming to, as it ever had been. Mama Linda, on her way. Her daughter, Rita, with the bullets Lynyrd'd written names on. Little Rose, with the life she carried, linking back to Sun Bear's grandfather's grandfather's grandfather, and beyond. Where she must go, Big Rose, ere this is over.

Erebus. Euphony. Eumenides. Eulogy. Dictionary words Lynyrd'd underlined in blue with a smiley face and star. That morning with the golden-pink San Juans lit up before them, numbers twelve and fourteen in their hands and the unlucky slot between, how they'd hoped. For a better world.

A world in order.

The pullet trembles in her hands, coos, bawks as it had that first morning in the floorboard of her man's truck. Its vent a mess. Blue-stained from the time before and the time before that.

It hurts her heart.

And what do you do, exactly, when hope begins to eat itself. To chew itself and swallow to a place no one can see? Out there in the field beyond good and evil and anything in between. No was, is, or will be.

Knocking on your door. Come neither as law nor man.

The broomstick thwacks the hen's right eye, golden then lidded. And in death the thing explodes to life, furious in dying.

The rest sense danger, lift heads and are quiet.

When she is still, Big Rose lifts her by the clawed feet, drops her in the dirt outside the pen, and so starts the pile. It is not a thing she would ever wish upon another, nor a collection of images and sounds, tastes and textures she'll never get shut of.

Like the sending home the spirit song, obnoxious and absurd, sung out of nowhere in the middle of the night.

30.

All she'd ever wanted, Mama, was a way out. That Mormon boy back at Blanding High, a way out. And the one who came after, with the coal black hair hanging half down his back, whispering a love poem in one ear and a curse—or was it a promise?—in the other, a way out. Double dealing the river rats for Navajo permits on the San Juan, just get me the hell out already. Two Dog Washer with his Tucson connections and air-filled hypodermic jabbed into a horse vein, out. Explosives, a whole shitload up in that Marsh Pass cave, why not give it a roll? And now, Stoner. He'd sniffed her out. And when he said that she should think about Yazz, that it would be such a shame for him to end up in the same place as his daddy, well that hit home, just like he knew it would. He was her way out, Yazz. Her only way. And she'd told, the whole nine yards. Told and told and told. With every last ounce of her guile, she'd let him know what was what, who was in on it and how deep. And the backstory, the part about Paris and that wacky professor wiring Navajo bridge, how they'd lost their nerve and walked away from it at the last minute, so now the stuff was up in BC[1], where those archeologists had dug up that two-thousand-year-old mummy girl with her little mummy baby.

Where they were going now, where he was driving her. Uphill past Kayenta, the little sign that said Tsegi, all the house trailers burned so hot as to melt the steel frames they sat on.

Concrete stairs climbed up to nothing, all that was left of the old trading post. Right through the gate onto gravel. And there it was, dark mouth grinning.

The Washer boy's jalopy. Rita's. The Subaru.

Where he killed it, opened her door.

And all she'd ever wanted was a way out. And now, the ten-inch skinner cold against her thigh, she thought of her son and his father, about poetry and sunrise in the desert, and the quiet place inside she'd known before all this.

Stoner hadn't said a word when she told him. He had this look like a concrete slab, the view of Monument Valley encircling them. She'd ladled chili verde over scrambled eggs, good grated cheese and green salsa. Think about Yazzie, think about him.

"And they're going up there this second?" he said finally, into his coffee cup. "To dig it up?"

The early birds with their black masks stood staring, two couples, old geezers, their dollar bills folded under a water glass. Over there, where Little Rose Begay had her graduation picture taken, standing on a rib of red sandstone with Mitton Butte just off her right shoulder. Mama'd got an invitation in the mail and never responded. What do you say to Miss University of Utah Native American? How's it hanging, sis? Wanna dance the jingle dance. Trade eagle feathers. Let me braid your hair. My diploma framed with no mama in my name? My rèsumè? My *curriculum vitae*? Dressed in a bank vault's worth of turquoise and silver. Like hers didn't stink.

And now, look at her there, cross-legged on the blanket, vomiting into a red bandanna, with child if it was true. From that birdman that had brought Stoner speeding, a hundred miles an hour, trooper lights flashing, no siren.

Rita on the driver's side seat of her car, wide-eyed.

He'd opened the door for her, Stoner. Waited for her to get out. Think about Yazzie, he'd said.

With his cuffs and pistol, bear spray and knocker, walking

behind her just like they always do. A pretty May morning, hint of chill, the light warm and glowing. Maybe it would rain soon and Skeleton Mesa would bloom, scarlet gilia and cliff rose, penstemon and sego lily. New sage would fragrance the air and the pinyon nuts would form on limbs that threw shadows where ring-necked lizards crawled over bones of the long dead, nameless and forgotten.

They stood beside Rose on her blanket, that retching sound, the smell of it. Rita's door opens, her skirt ballooning to her knees when she got out. Joined them. And there they all were, the four of them. The other four up in BC[1], what it all came down to.

A face flashed up in the pocket, disappeared.

All on the same page now.

Each one of them with something hidden.

For Stoner, the age-old need to outrun his religion, all the Lees and Jensens and Christiansens and Hansens, Big Brother the Bishop, and that missionary time back in North Carolina where horny country girls had despised him. Laughed in his face then passed on their phone numbers, a rolled-up pair of panties, hold an index finger to their lips, just between you and me. A lifetime of growling dogs and do you want a biscuit, of lockdown with vodka-stinking Indians and claptrap small timers who couldn't spell their own names. Of never being able no matter what to please his warlock father because that just wasn't in the cards, was it? Of failing at every turn, his most celebrated moments, his biggest failures. The year of quarantine and what it did to the mind. And most of all, hidden inside is the very real love for his wife who has left him, with just cause, who he's written a letter to of late and is waiting and hoping and, yes, praying even, that she'll write back. That he can see her and say he's sorry and that he loves her and will forever. Tell her the holy name that lay hidden in his heart.

*   *   *

Rose Marie Begay had felt the life inside her since sunshine three days ago, when she first knew for sure that she would never be alone again. What it's like, that first knowing? Who had her father been and why? The man who'd worked the Aneth oil fields, loaded them in a car and driven off toward Dinnehotso, stop at the river bridge, get out with headlights splashed across the breadth of his back, challenge them all to race to Arizona on the other side. Their breaths hard in their chests, she'd beat him the last time, and he'd hugged her and said good enough. *Good enough.* What did that mean? Where had he gone? Why? Mama with the silver wire between her fingers, whipping mojos together at the end of the Kuya bridge, always with the same answer. Lose a life, gain a life. Inside her now, a part of everyone she has ever loved. The one up there in BC[1], him too.

Good enough.

Rita knows straight away that she might have to shoot this policeman, Stoner. That a bullet in the cylinder has his name on it, and that she could very well do such a thing. *Had* done such a thing. The last thing, sealed inside so long, unravels some, how the Mormons believed it was better to kill someone than let them live in sin, the Doctrine of Blood Atonement. She'd turned away from it, the Church, but it had weaseled itself into her for a while there, back when Rose was a girl and she'd do anything to protect her child. Wouldn't she? Anything at all. There'd be consequences, Sister Rita knows. But if she has to shoot him, she will.

Just a little off his right shoulder, Mama could take him from the side. If she had to, she could. Rita's giving her the look. Sick Rose aglow. One of them had shown face up above.

They know.

She can't see Stoner's eyes, read them. If Big Rose was here, she'd turn him around—they'd had words earlier, *you here as a cop or a man?* She'd asked him that, some balls. And he didn't have an answer for that, did he?

Tsegi Canyon, and all of the names it had been known by throughout time and before there was time, upside down mountain, place among the rocks, Canyon de Chelly, Bone House, Skeleton Dancing, Canyon de Muerte, the dry husks of words that are no more for the living, was a piece of this earth with a feel to it, a current both beautiful and violent and something else that turned the inner dial toward it. There before road was graded over footpaths that wound up to Pueblo Cliff House, and the masoned stone laid over the cist graves of those who'd come before, whose bodies were sewn into death cloths kept immaculate through the long journey by cool, dry air, and the care with which they'd been sung into that last sleep.

Water came rippling, the sharp smell of sulfur. How light plays on stone. Unseen, but sensed. Felt. A realness to react toward, against. Out in the field beyond good or bad, here or there, the raven call that turns the man's head, because one he loves makes that sound. What all this comes to.

Love.

A way in, a way out. Four of them here, and four of them there. Each on the verge. Always a moment rocketing toward us, what we're headed toward. Neither dark nor light. How the hound had known him.

Stoner. Stone man.

All of this in the braided moment before the percussive wallop. When the raven traces shadow on the cliff wall, makes the sound that turns the man's head. How a holy man tells the medicine story, looping back to the same moments, reemphasizing this one then that, winding and unwinding. A white fingernail of flower moon in blue sky. Something familiar about the blanket where the girl sits retching, the raven black on her shoulder. Mixed with the sharp sulfur smell.

Raven. Moon. Blanket. Knife. Gun.

Bear spray.

Above, the mouth of cave explodes.

Rocks, no, boulders, make a river rolling, dragging sound from the vacuum. Stoner feels fine dust on his face, his eyes, before he tastes it. There is the urge to fall to the ground and cover the head, which they all do. Then it's quiet, and except for the dust and lone rock falling, over.

Big Cave One's not there anymore. Other than that, and the sudden awareness of ringing in the ears, the world is the same, only different. He tells the women to stay down, it might not all have gone at once.

No, Little Rose says, her voice like heartbreak.

No!

Stoner's heard the sound before, from his own mouth.

31.

He'd tricked her home, of course he had, Kidding. Up Chinle, he'd followed the Comb south and west, unwarps and scree-scattered climbs wound into the mouths of caves where cliff dwellers had lived on top of their predecessor's graves, sometimes molesting them, sometimes not. When the heart is right, a site will open itself to you, the cave cemeteries with their cists dug into hardpan where the mummified remains sometimes yielded and let themselves be seen. By the time he hit Kayenta and re-provisioned for the final leg of field work, 1916, he'd seen about all the land had to throw at him. Little surprised Kidding. The man who'd bathed naked early that fall off the San Juan, who'd offered tobacco and prayed that he might do things in a good way before Baseball Man and Star Woman, who'd sat at the tablestone and held the hammer stone in his right hand, who'd beheld the ticked triangle of pottery and couldn't bear to take it, who'd envisioned it as a piece of forever that would fit exactly in his daughter's hand, he was gone. In his place, who Kidding had become, the signature at one end of the shipments east to the Peabody, his notes accompanying the black and white photographs, directions on what the party'd left behind for the next. Wife and daughter's letters awaited him, postmarked and smelling of the insides of their wrists. His reply was hurried: *happy half birthday, yes, I'm taking care of myself, until fall, love.*

Big Cave One, he hadn't seen it coming, Kidding.

Literally, it was invisible, the cliff face blank as a sand dune at a distance. You could stare straight at it and not see. More than once he had. Like the antelope outside the train window when he'd first come west. Look out on the ocean of sage and sky and there was nothing, *nada y nada*. Then, an ear flicked, a tail, a hundred would materialize. This was like that, BC¹.

White dots lined the wall a foot off the cave floor. A trace of red run through them. Wide shouldered anthromorphs caught lantern light on the walls, horizontal lines glyphed above their heads, and some sort of line chiseled from the left eye back into space. Seeing the past? Future? Did they have such concepts? Who knew what they thought? Two thousand, three thousand years from when Kidding's size eleven feet first tread upon this dirt, breathed the air, his trowel blade ringing off the cave wall.

And it faced north, so the chill remained. The light was funny. And it felt for the world like someone was watching him dig, alien eyes, armed to the teeth with cold stone points and flesh scrapers, the carved boomerang clubs and beautifully made atlatls, fine bladed knives and knapped hatchet stones. Give him the willies even after all he'd laid eyes on. Dice made from human teeth. Always a skull grinning in the kiva ventilators. Facing outward. For who knows what? Mummies of babies lashed to cradles, fine umbilical pads lashed cross their navels with cord made of human hair.

A white dog on a mound of flies.

The bodies always wrapped in fur string blankets, the women in aprons. Encased in woven bags, one piece over the head, the other up from the feet, sewed in the middle with yucca thread.

Some body parts had been dragged out by cave rats. The cliff dwellers dug up whatever they could find. Skin bagsful of perfect corn. Digging sticks. Caches of points. The teeth dice.

Ventilator skulls.

Green stones laced intricately into hair bobs. Rock-a-bye-baby in the tree top. Hundred-yard-long rabbit nets sound as the day they were made. Love medicine. Mojo.

Kidding was by no means the first thief. Nor the last.

And this day, toward the end of it, when names for days had lost their salt and he'd reached the driest portion of the cold cave, mummies so well-preserved that the pores of the skin still breathed, their tresses of hair immaculately braided and bobbed.

His trowel rang with the first touch.

Kerosene from the lantern on the lip of the cist turned his stomach just a little, the willies full on him now, a note hummed by the toothless cave mouth, facing north, the wrong way. He'd sent their bodies by the trainload east to Peabody where they were numbered, catalogued, stored and displayed, some of them. Studied and calculated for age and sex, diet and disease. Cause of death. Gum disease and decay. Their belongings and dogs and garments, teeth dice rolled to snake eyes. And now, this second in BC[1], on the South Comb just off Marsh Pass, on a day with no name though he'd remember it as Sunday, when the cave mouth moaned a note he'd never heard and his best trowel sang out the rebirth of his teenage bride with her firstborn lashed to a lap cradle, he'd make the find that would catapult him to fame and fortune and the sad grave on the hill where he'd finally make peace.

He dug her out gently. Whisked dust from her shroud with a fine paintbrush. Blew little puffs of breath on undressed eyelids, the face. The thrill fully on him. He'd smoke later, sip single malt, replay the moment.

And the shock.

For tied around her neck was a thing no man had ever seen since the time of Christ and before. Magically sustained and kept perfect. Holy. Far-seeing. Her trophy.

The zenith of his work, his life, his soul, even. How his hands shook when he touched it, lightly, the way one holds a child's hand. Thinking *what on earth?*

Later, out under the good sun, and thereafter, in the lab under bright artificial light, he'd examine then analyze his find, compose *Kidding, A.V. 1919. Archeological Explorations of Northeastern Arizona. Bulletin 65, Bureau of American Ethnology. Washington, 1919.*

CEREMONIAL OBJECTS
"Scalp"

This object was found around the shoulders of the "mummy" in Cist 16, Cave I (p. 87, a,b). It is the entire head skin of an adult, with the hair carefully dressed. In its preparation the scalp proper, including the ears, was removed from the skull in one piece: the face to mouth in another: and the chin with the lower cheeks in a third. After curing, the three sections were sewed together again, one seam running across the forehead and one down each side in front of the ears; the horizontal seam which joins the upper and lower face pieces crosses the region of the mouth, but the skin along this sewing has been so trimmed, probably in order to insure a straight seam, that no sign of the lips remains. The eyes and nose, though shriveled, are plainly recognizable; the eyebrow and eyelash hairs are still in position. Although thorough examination under the brittle side bobs is impossible, one can make out the shrunken ears; through the lobe of each there runs a bit of yucca string, the attachment cords presumably for pendants that have now disappeared. The face has been colored rather elaborately: the "part" and tonsure of hair are painted with a pasty, greenish-white pigment; up the center of the "part" and across the tonsure runs a narrow streak of yellow. Just under the forehead seam there is a thin, horizontal band of red. From this to a line drawn across the face half an inch below the eyes is a zone of white. A band left in the natural color of the skin extends from here to just below the nostrils, whence to the bottom of the white paint is continuous, except for a broad median band of red running downward from the mouth seam.

Rove through two small holes in the tonsure is a narrow thong for suspension. In this part of the scalp there is a short rent carefully sewed up, probably a wound or cut made in skinning.

This interesting specimen seems to have been prepared and used as a trophy. The dressing of the hair was probably done after the skin was cured; its arrangement is peculiar and, so far as we know, is not similar to any known style used in recent times in the Plateau. The head was presumably that of an enemy, though there is no way of telling whether it was an enemy of the same or of a different stock. (*Archeological Explorations in Northeastern Arizona.* Alfred V. Kidder and Samuel J. Guernsey. Smithsonian Institution, Washington D.C., 1919. p. 190-191).

By 1300 they were all gone, these people, starved, fled to the Hopi, death by thirst. All that was left of their religion was in the dirt, on stone walls, Star Woman, the teen mother and child. Hopi girls wore their hair in bobs, for the Corn Maiden coming of age ceremony, they did. Yet studies of Southwest Anasazi, say the Kayenta variety, have yet to ascertain a direct link between the Hopi mesas and said tribe, beyond an apparent causal relationship regarding dramatic population increase on 1st, 2nd, and 3rd Mesas during the period between 1300 and 1600. Laguna Creek immigrants surely found their way to Isleta Pueblo where they chewed scalps, the Tewa women, named them *po se e*, "little mists." Spat the blood-juice on clay they formed into cakes with their fingers, fed them to braves to cure loneliness and longing.

The thought went through him, how the flesh must have felt between the teeth, the hair, how a cavity tastes when let go too long, aroma of decay on the tongue.

Symbols of fertility and well-being, maybe. Water, the green stripe, all things living. Making the enemy a member of the tribe, bringer of water, *po se e*.

During that time the Hopi began to practice socio-norms heretofore unknown to the mesas, a corn society formed and curative times and ceremonies aligned with seasonal holy days, the equinoxes, for instance, when footraces occurred from plaza to plaza, runnings unheard of before. The *po se e* laced to the tip of a pinyon pole, dark lock braided with blood red cloth and owl feather, carried high above the head on race war day, skin pliant and yielding in the solstice breeze. Ravens *caw caw* from the far shadow, riding ice air through the mouth moan where he tricks from her all she has to give, more. And before it rains, the scalp cries.

No need for the trowel now, Kidding's shaking had given way and he worked slowly, the undressed mummy revealing all, his eyes fully adjusted to the dark, he let the kerosene burn out, sorted it out by the light natural to Big Cave One. Filtering from somewhere above and behind, there must be a window of some kind. A way in. Out. Where the sound came from, it dawned on him.

The moan he'd neither shake nor live down.

Not in this lifetime.

Still, the light that fell on the bodies before him, on his own hands at work, had a source, surely it did. Some false entrance, or trick of the cave walls.

A moment of light.

PART THREE

PART THREE

32.

One cave over, Yazzie assured her on their way out, was Sunflower Cave, where they'd dug up a fur-lined basket of painted sunflowers carved from wood fresh and clean as if made yesterday. It was a good sign him saying that, because Daddy'd called her Hardy Sunflower in that last long letter before the fall, and they'd burst up outside his study window in spring after the rains. Were blooming there no doubt this second, in the city where she was born in January, named for the god that looks forward and back, future to past from the space of the present. Of course they'd seen Stoner from the mouth of the cave, Linda, Rose and her mom, the badge on his chest catching sun. A beautiful view really, *Tsegi*, place among the rocks, Monument Valley to the north, Valley of the Gods. Air humming through a back window as if the cave drew breath. Yazzie showed them, just the right size to crawl through, the way out.

It sticks with her, the sunflowers, as fresh and clean as the day there were made. Carved, painted, buried in a cave for millennium. Behind them, the cave's not there anymore. No sign of it, nor what happened there like it's a dream suddenly waked up from and not remembered, really, just the loose threads waving in the periphery.

It was like that.

Edgar'd dragged something out the invisible window.

They'd run a ways, crouched low against the rocks. That's sun-flower cave, right over there, Yazzie'd said, and that's when the sound came, the shaking. A raven screamed from the cliff face when it was done. There'd been spraypaint inside, horrible stuff. She'd left her keys in the car, the guitar and Igloo cooler with one of mom's Turkey sandwiches still wrapped in cello-phane. Lemonades on ice. Who'd driven cross country from Florida across Georgia, Mississippi into south Arkansas, north to Solgahatchia—the Trail of Tears. Lanty, where the family cemetery gate had let out a squeal, the light rain had fallen when dogs were barking and the air smelled of burnt tires.

Watch out for Stoner, Daddy'd written. *Heyduke lives*.

The second thing, a mystery.

If you'll just get me out of this, she remembered thinking, though to whom the thought was aimed was beyond Luce Harvell, twenty-three that spring, on the heels of teaching Haitian kids to read in south Florida, where she'd sometimes drive to the landfill because it had a slight hill to it, so she could think of home where there were mountains and snow. The last time there she'd driven a back way home past 4th Ave and the City Cemetery, where a Mexican funeral was going on in a plot just off the road with the foothills shining. A brass band, the silver horns flashing, was playing Dixieland jazz, a big tuba that seemed to float above tombstones on its own honk-honking, then the sweet Spanish voices singing *oh when the saints, come marching in*, and she'd pulled over, rolled her windows down and wept and wept with that sorrow mixed with joy that was the sweet sad music of this world her father'd hummed to her in the hour of her birth. One of them met eyes with her and smiled.

Just to prove it was true. Sideways in time.

There'd been a lone gunshot below. Edgar'd started cry-ing, and she'd hugged him and said it would be alright. They'd walked toward the sound, her and Yazzie, blue-eyed Louie, Mr. Paris.

Had come walking up on Officer Stoner and Rita with the pistol still in her hand, Linda, and Rose Marie, who'd reclined the passenger seat of the Sube far as it would go, motioned for Edgar to get in, which he did. No one noticed them, not Stoner nor Rita nor Mama, except in an out of the corner of the eye kind of way. Like they ghost-walked in between a seam in time. Out there, they were having a serious talk, the three of them, Rita waiving that big pistol this way and that. Stoner nodding. The three of them making a triangle.

The keys were in the ignition. She got in, started it, shifted into reverse and backed out. From his car, Louie waved, said bye. Yazz saluted, that crooked Indian grin. And they drove away. Just like that. The boys one way, Luce the other, east and west.

Making their getaway.

Into the land of the Woolly-headed Washers, what Mr. Paris said. Where there were others like them, children born of mothers who'd been brought here, to Arizona, under false pretense and run away. Boys and girls long grown into men and women. And by now those children would have children, and those children children, maybe. A vast woolly-headed feral people who wouldn't know each other from Adam.

Toward these they drove.

As if it was possible to slip from one world to the other. All that baggage back behind, the jobs teaching kids who knew the Haitian word for *tree*, for *bread*, for *life* and *death*. *Birdhouse*.

Schoolyards where your grandmother'd buried the placenta you were born in so you'd come back, racing across the river bridge with its boatman and two-headed dog. The pile of dead chickens had grown high in the dirt yard where sat the sad truck with expired tags stuck on an Arkansas plate that read DMF 936. Tools for grave digging in the bed. Bits of bugs from the Natural State stuck on the front grill, atlas jammed under the driver's seat, Arkansas and Arizona on pages that faced each other.

From whence they had not packed clothes nor said good-bye. Their people back there beckoning. The white flag. Caught unawares at the cool spring where they sipped before the run at Nevada which fell away to the blue door of ocean and all that it signified.

Hope, freedom, life and love.

The pursuit of happiness.

Wasn't that what they were all after, the Indians and Arkies, Stoner and his bride of the secret holy name. That was it, *pursuit*. All of them in the hunt.

Desire renewed through the ages.

Nameless, wordless, what they were after.

Heaven and earth, home.

By Tuba City, Mr. Paris has discovered the D-28 mewing on the seat beside him, and if Rose doesn't pee this second, she's going to die.

"Of course not really," she smiled. "I just have to go."

Luce hits a truckstop that Edgar recognizes as having stopped at before. "They have good biscuits," he said. And, "Man, this is a sweet guitar."

They fuel up, go, buy ham and cheese biscuits. Paris kicks the tires. They fill all Luce's water bottles and an empty orange juice jug from the cooler. Middle of the day in May, they pull into the shade of a semi-trailer, eat in silence. Deciding.

If you don't want, take to Mr. Edgar Paris in Dinnehotso, Arizona, what he'd written. Of course, he wouldn't take it. "Of course, I can't." And when he said *can't*, it rhymed with *paint*.

How Daddy'd said it, she remembered. Strange how you go on hearing their voices, talking from the interstellar void in the middle of dreams. Mom would be worried about her—she should call.

No such thing as can't, he'd said. *Can't never did anything*.

The semi's black, a long-nose Peterbilt. The driver meets their eyes before climbing into the cab of the truck that, Luce realizes, is still running, the way Daddy's daddy'd left his all night outside whatever rent house they lived in in those Lonoke County days of his rocky upbringing. Grandfather O.W. All that.

When the truck gears up and moves, sun shines fiercely through the Subaru windows and Mr. Paris takes care to buckle the Martin back in its case. "Well?" Rose says.

"I don't know what he was thinking. Sending you with that." He follows the black semi with his eyes, onto the Interstate, the galaxy of radiant turn signals barely visible by the light of day.

33.

The way she'd said it, *no*, like her heart had broken that second, and no matter what happened for the rest of her days she'd never get over it, whatever'd gone off up on the hilltop where the cave mouth was no more, put him in the mind of the afternoon in Page, when he'd walked through the door he'd once carried her through to find that letter in Joanna's handwriting, the smell of her skin, and he'd known that one thing was over and another begun. She'd meant it with her whole heart, Little Rose, just like he had when he'd said it. And that connection with the Indian girl, sick and pregnant if Mama Linda be believed, touched him in some deep place he'd not known before. On all fours, he crawled to her side. The sob went through him like a spear. A raven screamed at them from cliff shadow.

He touched her elbow. Drew the handkerchief from his pocket and gave it to her. She took it. And in that moment, whatever else, he'd done right. No one could take it away from him. He'd done right.

It got real still, like church during a too long prayer.

From his periphery, Rita Begay said *goddamn*, real loud and sudden, and a pistol shot rang out between them. A pistol shot during a too long prayer. Well goddamn, how about that?

Mama Linda's on the ground behind them, her breath ragged. He hears her moving like a snake. He'd pushed her too far, Stoner had. The business about Archie. Telling her to think about her son. The hideout knife strapped to her thigh no doubt sharp enough to shave skin. And Rita with a pistol, where'd that come from? The girl's man had blown himself to kingdom come up there, probably, Yazz and the Washer kid, the Harvell girl whose Subaru with Florida plates is parked on open road behind them.

She loved the Arkie, Little Rose. Just like he loved Joanna. It was all the same thing for Indians and Arkies, Saints and sinners, the language of love.

"Rose," Rita said. *"Rose?"*

Up on the hill, nothing moved. Just a few rocks settling. It was a big one, her pistol.

She sobbed, said, "I'm okay, mama."

Behind him, the snake, her scales swishing sand, the knife unsheathed already, about to draw blood.

Rita with the draw on him, Mama cutthroat at his shoulder, a split second when Stoner could take them both out with bear spray, his right hand not three inches from the canister on his hip, godawful stuff that took the sight and breath so you'd think they'd never come back.

Nothing shaking up on the hill.

Just the four of them and the moment, each revealing what had been concealed—gun, knife, bear spray, the child kicking in her womb, fatherless now, like he'd always been, black sheep Stoner.

"Don't," Rose said. "Don't, Mama."

She held both hands palm up, between him and her mother, one of them, the other freezing Linda.

"Stop it."

Rita lowers the hog leg—just enough. He feels Mama with the skinner behind him. She could lift his scalp from back there, if not for Rose.

Stoner says, "Ladies." A stupid thing.

Raven caw-caws from the cliff shadow, the sound Joanna could make. She'd received his letter by now, no doubt, was deciding. And why on earth is he thinking of her at a moment like this, a whole lot in the balance.

"Officer Stoner," Rita said.

He sat there, beside her daughter. The spray'd get up her nostrils, mist her eyes, and so the baby'd have to deal with it, and he's not sure what would happen with that. Blindness, maybe. Skin defects.

"Mrs. Begay."

"Let's talk."

Not going to happen, the pepper spray.

"Let's do."

A pillar of red dust rises before them, and Mr. Raven's putting on a show, dipsy-doodling it and going *caw-caw-caw*, sun purpling its wings. Hair on the back of his neck stands up, and there's a chill come down from BC¹, which is no more.

"Mama?" Stoner says. "You okay back there?"

No sound save the hiss.

"I'm taking her to the car. If it's okay. Might be more up there."

Rita's pistol barrel wagged yes. Took the blanket with him, covered her in the Harvell girl's passenger seat, reclined, that sob. When he came back, they made a triangle—Mama, Stoner, Rita Begay. Already, it's been a morning, a day to hang your hat on. More on the way, ole hog leg on Rita's lap, the one dark eye. The slight bulge of Linda's skinner on her left thigh, and the whole deal ready to roll from Stoner's holster belt. The fool-clown crow turning somersaults in the red dust rising. And they'd made a triangle, two women and the man.

"You first," Rita said.

He'd seen a piece of pottery once, a shard, over off Comb Ridge, a black ticked triangle painted against a white background, repeating, so if you drew the connections out past the shard, it went on forever. He'd left it where he found it, had learned that much about Indian mojo from being starved in the backwoods by the company his father the warlock had hired to straighten his ass out. How he said it, "straighten your ass out." Before he became an Elder, met Joanne, had his heart broken, lived in the Jacob Lake lockdown with Brother Kavapulu and tribe.

His first days out in the real world, what brought him here.

What to do hits him and he does not hesitate, Stoner. Unbuckles the holster with its Colt .45 Auto and plastic cuffs, stunner and spray, wooden knocker and spare clips. Hefts it into the dirt between them, the centroid, center of their mass.

"Maybe we should disarm," Stoner said.

Time's gone saucy on them. Who knows? Mama Linda laughs, a rueful sound, though he's not sure that's the right word. Joanna was the poet in the family, she'd describe it some other way. It's a wicked laugh, Mama's.

A fillet knife lands on top of Stoner's weapons, the kind made in Ireland he'd used for filleting trout on the Green, browns the length of his calf, catch fifty in a day.

In the car, Little Rose's quit crying. Sits upright, paying attention to something invisible from his vertex in the triangle's space.

"Kuya," Rita says.

"Come again." Mama to his left, Rita to his right. The girl back behind his back the Orthocenter? It had once come easy to him, angles. The geometry of love.

"The world out of balance." Rita lays a red bandanna from her skirt on the sand in front of her, sets the ebony-handled revolver on its side, barrel end pointed circumcenter.

The raven squawks, flap flaps over the rise. Other fish to fry.

"I guess it is," Stoner said.

"You tell him all?"

Rita rubs her dark hands together, holds them out like there's a campfire burning between them. Stoner remembers the styro in the cruiser's back seat, filled with leftover biscuits and gravy from the View buffet. He should give them to the girl, settle her stomach. Fetch a warm ginger ale from the carton in the trunk, do her right.

Mama says, "Yeah. Just about."

"That's Louie's ride. What's it doing here?"

Rita nods to where the cave should have been, and maybe the thought starts to form between them, the collective vision of what had happened and why and what it meant for them and their lives from there on out. How they'd explain it, triangulate it, the way the geometers of old could measure approximate distance to the sun and stars, calculate from the angles and get it damn near close to right. Knowledge that had been lost when Christians burned the libraries at Athens and Rome, the wisdom of the world hurled into the pit of the Dark Ages, with shining residue secreted in Persia, Baghdad, the silk and spice road, so that stars bore their names, and the flat sun circled an earth bloated in the ether of ignorance.

Joanna-talk chattering in his brain—what's wrong with him, Stoner? He'd said she should think about her son, Yazzie, the only thing Archie'd ever touched that she hadn't thrown away.

Nodded up to the hillside, where the cave ought to be. The pillar of dust rising where the raven had somersaulted before sighting something else to do violence to, that *caw-caw-caw* of Jo's loud and clear. She'd had one tattooed on her right shoulder, so a river guide who rowed with a blow-up doll as passenger had raised his brows while rolling a cigarette from loose tobacco, said, "*Oy*, in some cultures the raven is a bad omen, you know, ripping the eyeballs out the heads of young dead soldiers on the battlefield."

Why does she come to him now, in the thick of it? The women straddle either end of the vertices running west to east, or east to west, depending. To his left, BC¹, supposed to be. Right, Tsegi. Behind him, the Subaru with Florida plates, Little Rose all eyes now, sniffing, the Indian in her on full alert.

Mama Linda to his left, Rita to his right. Their collective weaponry the center of mass. Time squirrely, all wrong. Like the time him and Joanna'd taken peyote, her idea, some Navajo prayer bullshit, send smoke signals to the other side.

There's water in the cruiser. Medicine. Biscuits and gravy in a styro box. They sit in a triangle, each on a point. And the triangle fits into a circle shot through with lines called legs.

The sound of a car crunching gravel, the engine running, missing a little, slap some new plugs in there, fix her up. Doors open and shut, and the car is leaving, crunching away. Gone.

"So you here as a man or cop?" Big Rose, behind his back, using Joanna's words on him.

She steps through, sits so they're two triangles now. A diamond. They're all likely dead up there. On the hillside. All that dynamite gone off. Should be digging them out. Search and rescue. Time is precious.

She had fresh blood on her Nikes, Big Rose. Sat cross-legged looking at him, eyes black like the inside of a light socket. A throat clears behind him and somebody spits. Lynyrd, whose Indian name was unspeakable.

"It was a gas explosion up there. Wasn't it," Rose said. "That methane seep. Shouldn't a'been smoking. Fool kids."

Four against one, Lynyrd behind his back. That's when he hears it, the low growl. Dog, they've brought the goddamn dog.

Blood's spattered on her face and neck, Big Rose. Not unlike war paint. She had Sun Bear's medicine in her veins, real-deal Indian stuff. Was her made time squishy, the methane seep, smoking, the explosion.

"We should go up there and dig them out," Stoner said. "Might be one of them alive."

Over their head, the jet-black raven jeers. Somersaults into the pillar of dust. Growls.

He'd heard the birds could talk, but *growl?*

34.

Daddy was thirty-three the year they came west, sort of a holy number for a man born on Christmas Day though what did she know about it? All that Bible business with its holy star and wise men and little baby born in a manger. Down in Tucson, when she'd run away from home that time with Jackson Tripp and hooked up with her dwarf uncle, he'd taken her to Mission San Xavier de Bac where grandmother Josephine had once prayed to Mary for the birth of the son that would fly to her on Christmas morning, when she'd hemorrhaged and the surgeon kept walking out of the waiting room and saying the mother wouldn't make it and then, the baby won't make it, but of course they both did, or she wouldn't be here, Luce Harvell. And on a barred hilltop cave outside, a bronze plaque said *Here appeared the Blessed Virgin who intercedes for us with Christ the King.* She'd been twenty that day, Josephine. And daddy's father'd given her pearl earrings, maybe they were pearl, for her birthday, and she'd left them there for Mary with the prayer: *please intercede for us, protect my son, talk to Him for us.* And when Davy'd taken her up the hillside path, with golden Mexico just to the south and Mt. Lemon gleaming snow-capped to the north, they glittered there, set in silver at the foot of the plaque. She'd kissed them, said thank you, and left them be. Maybe they were the same ones. Maybe.

Mom's text says *call me, I'm worried.*

Luce replies: *driving now, soon as I stop.*

In the truck stop parking lot, they'd decided. Give it some time. Let things settle. Keep their heads down for a while. California? Why not?

Edgar and Rose are sacked out in the backseat, highway rolling on by. She'd met some of them, the Washers. They'd thrown a hootenanny for her at a Mexican restaurant, danced and drank tequila, and the old dwarf had taken her to the Catholic cemetery where her blood grandfather lay buried. His mother, and a kid buried under a stone lamb. She'd come away with his dog tags and a gift that she was not to open until she was way gone. *Way gone*, she remembered thinking. What on earth.

Inside, six crisp fifties lay inside the graduation card that had never been mailed. The Washers had signed, wished daddy their love, left phone numbers and maps and invitations to visit. Xs marked stayover spots. There was a photo, a framed three by five of the three of them—Josephine, daddy in the middle, and the father he never met.

Not ever save as a baby.

What must that not knowing be like?

She'll need maternity clothes, Rose. To see a doctor from time to time. Eat right. Get exercise. The ocean air would be good for her. Isn't that what they said?

Story was her grandfather Buddy had tricked Josephine into leaving Arkansas with a story about how he'd been married before, and had a baby that quit talking because the mommy'd been hit by a truck and killed. And it so needed another mommy, wouldn't she please come help. So by the time they hit the big heart of Texas she'd believed herself the mother of all lost children, and her heart was big for the child that did not yet exist.

Tricked by a lie. By her heart.

Mom said, *Where are you now? Why won't you answer?*
In a minute, she said. *California, Just barely.*
What on earth for?

What on earth for. The hundred-dollar question. What is it
that has compelled her to come this way? She has a job, back
there somewhere she does. Teaching Haitian kids to read books
about white people, their parents mowing lawns and poisoning
bugs and reroofing wind-damaged condos. Pouring the man's
concrete and framing new apartment complexes to replace
the ones that have rotted down. Jobs her father had grown up
doing, what sent him to school and kept him there. History had
been rich enough ground for him to unearth what he needed
to make a living, send her to school, pay for a house, braces,
dental, life insurance, new cars and trucks when they needed
them. Drive up to a gas pump and fill the damn tank. Buy four
new tires at a time. Steak when he wanted. Vacation in Spain.
Cabo. British Columbia. Arkansas only once after Mom Dee
died, a VRBO off Lake Ouachita where he'd once spent weeks
at a time in summer with his maternal grandfather, running tro-
tlines for catfish, bathing naked in a cove where the one-legged
man would climb on a piling so it looked like he walked on
water. Pick okra, Big Boys from the garden, butternut squash,
get away from Josephine and O.W. trying to kill each other.
Hadn't she heard it all. Hadn't she.

What else for people like that to do but go west. Clean
slate. Everything about to come full circle. A coast where the
spent sun fell into the sea, pulled you toward it, kept pulling.

Her, too.

Daddy's fight with the Mormons was in her blood just like
his. How could it not be? She was a Poteet only one generation
removed from him, and wasn't that a name written on one of
the sticks of dynamite they'd blown to kingdom come back
there at Tsegi? And weren't they walking to California, nearly
to the Nevada line when they got waylaid. Tricked by the white

flag at a spring near Mountain Meadows? It wasn't her fight, no. But she wasn't free and clear of it either. And maybe, now that all the names Daddy and Edgar had wired to the bridge once named for the man executed for the deed had blown up, it was time to finish the journey, make it to the ocean, breathe it in and turn loose.

She didn't think of it just like that, not in those words, Luce, more of a feeling, this way instead of that, just like all the choices to be made on this earth.

Why?

Lose a life, gain a life.

"You okay up there?"

She nods to Edgar in the rearview. "Yeah."

"Where we at?"

"California," she said. "Just barely."

A telephone pole tall cowboy with a blue hat says *Las Vegas, 100 Miles*, and *World's Largest Steak: Free If You Can Eat It All*. The sun throws the cowboy's shadow, a long day, so much to process, lay low, keep their heads down. They needed gas. A place to rest. But they hadn't really thought that through, had they? Were they wanted? Accessory to the crime? Fleeing from an officer of the law? They had neither guns nor weed, and very little money save the nearly maxed credit card in the river wallet in the center console she'd once written her name on with a black sharpie, Daddy's. How it came to her, who knows.

"Rose. We're in California. Look."

She sees her in the rearview. Pretty, a flash of smile. "I could do it," she says. "I could eat that steak."

She turns the air off, cracks the windows. The radio's been on a Christian station out of Kingman, Jesus this and Jesus that, what had got her thinking to begin with. Daddy and Mom coming west when he was thirty-three, the year Christ was crucified. He'd tell the story over Easter ham and deviled eggs every year, the donkey with a cross on its back, palm fronds,

Pontius Pilot and Barabbas, *crucify him, crucify him.* The two thieves, one on either side. Today you will walk with me in Paradise. How they'd stage a Styrofoam ball painted to look like a boulder in front of a closet made to look like a tomb at First Baptist in Lonoke for resurrection service. Sounds of the boulder being rolled aside were amplified over loud speakers as a stunned Mary in a very southern accent said, *He is risen, He is risen.* And the congregation burst out with *Up from The Ground He Arose!* his favorite part. Pass around the silver trays of crumbled saltines, the little shot glasses filled with bitter grape juice—partake of the body and blood. *He Arose! He Arose! Hallelujah Christ Arose.*

Three sheets to the wind, he'd sing it from the end of the table, as if he meant it with his whole heart. As if true.

"Let's do it," Rose says. "Let's go scarf that steak."

35.

For Yazz and Louie Washer, the pile of dead chickens adds a layer of riddle to a day that has come entirely undone. Someone has done violence to them, whacked their heads with an arm-length broomstick, left them lay in a bloody pile outside the coop. Big Rose'll shit. An egg lays beside one of the dead chickens, a pretty red hen with white feet. The black ones are hair-legged, scary things, eyes rolled back in crushed heads. They'd driven east to Dinnehotso fast as Louie's Impala would run, rods knocking and lifters tapping, it wasn't long for the world, Louie's car. Any second that cop about to run up on them with the bubblegum light flashing, haul them off to DT down in Flag, or worse. What they needed was to get the hell out of Dodge, Yazz and Louie. That was the plan. But the chickens. The goddamn chickens.

"Those are Rhode Island Reds," Louie said, pointing at a red one.

"*Duh*," Yazz said.

Lynyrd kept beer in a cooler on the back porch. The chickens demanded beer and serious thought, something had to be done, what? Yazz popped a PBR, not icy but okay as far as beer went.

Louie's dad knew somebody in Tucson. They could go there, drift on down into Mexico. Fuck it. Why not?

"We need money," Louie said, taking a sip. "Where'd we get the jack?"

The boys looked down on the poor, unlucky chickens.

"Duh," Yazz said. "We need money."

Thelma and Louise lay over in the shade of Edgar's truck. They'd seen the violence, knew the perpetrator. DMF 936, the Arkansas plates read, tags expired last February. No help.

Louie kicks the pile with the toe of his high tops. He wished for hooter, something with more bite than Lynyrd's warm beer. "Wonder if there's gas in'at truck?" Louie said. "I'm way low."

Across the yard, Thelma growled, low and mean.

"Duh. What's new," Yazz said.

They'd fought the one time. A bright Christmas morning when Louie's dad poured whiskey in his coffee, brought out the boxing gloves, said it was Boxing Day in Canada, that they should go a few rounds, given the lack of presents and all, because they were shitass kids and deserved nothing more than lumps of coal and ass-whuppings, what he said. Louie and Yazz had strapped the gloves on and threw big haymakers at each other, rarely connecting, and soft when they did. Two-Dog watched from a kitchen chair dragged out to the front yard dirt, lacing coffee with whiskey in a jelly jar, shirtless, a red Santa hat with a dingy white ball hanging off it. They were like that, the Washers, whiskey for breakfast. After a while he got up, Louie's old man, said, "Give'em here," buried his big fists in a pair of gloves and motioned Louie to him. The first right had taken him off his feet, the eye swelling before he could even stand back up. Kept motioning him in, laying him out. *Bap, bap, bap.*

"Santa Claus's coming to town," Two-Dog sang. "Get up, boy."

He'd have knocked him toothless, if Yazz hadn't asked for the gloves.

"Kick some Indian ass? You want some of me?"

His pot belly lapped over his jean shorts. Big armed, he'd been arm-wrestling champ at Maryboy's Pool and Grill. Had killed a horse for Mama Linda, then threatened to snitch on her for the insurance money. Fucker.

Yazzie laced on the gloves. Christmas morning, a whiff of whiskey and blue sky and what in the world else is there to do for an Indian boy whose daddy's in prison. A lump of coal and an ass whupping.

"Yeah," Yazz said. "I do."

A boy he knew on Skeleton Mesa was a fancy dancer, coke bottle thick glasses and talked with a lisp, but goddamn could he ever move when the drumbeat came, throw feathered wings to the wind and those CDs flashing wild on his chest, go to town. How a boxer moves.

Yazzie danced a circle around Two-Dog, throwing long-distance zingers that wouldn't hurt a fly. Louie's eye was purple now, fat-lipped. His mother's face appeared behind the busted out storm window, disappeared.

The shock of the first blow *yaw-yawed* through Yazzie's bones, numb, the light bright. The second one caught him just below the sternum, took his breath, bent him over.

Washer waded in, about to throw the uppercut that would clean Yazzie's clock. A step too late. Yazz stood up hard, brought his head whizzing up under Two-Dog's chin, the crunch of teeth breaking.

Louie's daddy stood there looking, that sideways whiskey grin. He opened his mouth, stuck out the tongue which missed its bloody tip.

"Gooth mooth, Yathie," he said, walked back to his kitchen chair. "Merry gothdamn Cwithmath."

The pile of dead chickens moved. Louie kicked it, and then it had moved. Just like that. And up jumped a black hen with a smashed beak that flapped its wings to Jesus and hauled ass between them so Yazzie nearly shit his pants, and maybe did, through he'd never say so, would he?

Ran down the gravel drive and across the road to Laguna

Creek, kept on running that chicken, making its getaway, runaway chicken, keep on going. It was a good sign, the boys decided, the resurrected chicken running for its life, freedom, into the land of the woolly-headed Washers.

Poor people know the bread trick.

How to carry a couple slices of white Wonder with the green length of hose, have it at the ready when you screw the gas cap off whatever automobile you're about to siphon, because always, always, after those first two or three hard sucks comes a sudden mouthful, and if you're lucky, which you never are, you don't swallow. And just let me tell you, ain't nothing light up your ass like a swallowed mouthful of unleaded, fossil sunlight, Texas Tea. Burn you right down to your core. That's where the white bread comes in. Take a slice out of the little baggie Mama used to slide on under your socks—Indian snow boots—squeeze it into a ball, shove it in and chew, about the only thing on earth'll soak up the gas, take it out of your mouth, if not your belly. Sixteen kinds of high, already, whoa Mama. Lynyrd had taught him the trick at the WE TOTE THE NOTE used car lot where they kept their junkers empty as possible and were always having to siphon up a half gallon or two. He knew the bread trick, Yazz. And needed it this morning, boy did he ever.

Edgar's truck was a Chevy half-ton, solid as a rock with a column shifter and firm clutch, a key under the DSM, which Yazz knew about from shuttling river rat rigs Bluff to Mexican Hat, old man Valle's operation which Mama had some skin in. He'd worked one whole season, Yazz, stealing their phone chargers and CDs, Highway to Hell, one of them, his bball, the autographed Spaulding kind, a dime bag here and there, whiskey under the seat, cigs, a four-way lug wrench and WD-40. They came off the river too stoned to notice, gas tanks on the light side, where's the spare sunglasses. What happened to AC-DC?

Key under the driver's side mat, fucking A. Half a tank it says when he turns the ignition. Well *hoe down*. Arkansas plates, expired in February. No goddamn problem, turning a 2 into a 9, kiddo stuff.

Louie climbed in the open passenger's side reached under the seat and bingo, Old Crow, a swallow left, another of Fireball. Behind the seat, a Woodsmaster .30-ought six, Model 742 in a zip case, full box of silver tip shells, magnums. Clip loaded, one in the chamber. The chicken had been good luck. Lucky fucking chicken.

"Why not just take the son of a bitch?" He'd swallowed a mouthful while siphoning Edgar's gas, run for a slice of Big Rose's white bread which Thelma'd hog-gobbled when he spit it out.

"Dad won't like it, we get caught."

His belch fills the cab, you could light it. "Who's getting caught?"

Louie screws the cap off the Fireball, sniffs. Takes a knock and spits it out, right on the floorboard.

"Don't waste it," Yazz says. "Let me see that gun."

"Maybe they'll be looking for it. This truck."

Yazz grips the checkered forestock, whistles. "*Duh*."

You could smell him, bird man.

There were tools in the bed under the camper shell, shovels and rakes and a bucketful of trowels and edgers, a magnesium hand float. Post hole diggers and a socket wrench set."

"*Duh* what?"

"Give me a charge of that. Won't need it where he's going. Stone man gets ahold of him. Fucker has a 3 x 9 scope on it with a wide lens. Jesus."

"Two-Dog'll kill me."

In his head, it's already his, the Chevy, deer rifle and hand tools. What it gets for making him swallow gas. "Fut do-dog," Yazzie says, the Fireball mixed with gasoline now. "Follow me to Maryboy's. We'll leave yours there. Take the gas. They'll think somebody kidnapped us. Happens to Indians all the time."

Louie Washer pushes the door shut from the outside. "It have a player?"

"Killer," Yazz says.

"You sure?"

"Blow your doors off."

"See if it'll start."

She fired right up on the third try, pumped it a little, smelled the gas. A little popcorn in the tailpipe. It was a good truck, Yazzie's.

"What about the chickens?"

"They'll think the thief did it. Whoever stole this truck."

"Us?"

"*Duh.* Of course, not us. Why'd we want to kill Rose's chickens?"

He was dense like that, sometimes, Washer.

36.

She'd loved Roger, yes she had, Joanna. And now, he was asking her back. Part of her wants nothing more than to put Vernal and her father and his temple and the whole nine yards of bullshit behind her back, and go back. To her ex. It happened. People did it all the time. She knew a professor whose mother had divorced and remarried the same man three times so they could never get their anniversaries right. He loved her more than anything on earth. And he was sorry. Boy, was he ever sorry. The hell with his Bishop brother, he'd tell her her secret name. That alone would be worth the price of admission. But the last thing, the note she'd left him on. Could she love one capable of that? Forgive? Countenance? The letter lay right now in the basket on top of the microwave, folded inside the National Geographic with the gladiator on its cover. *The Real Life Behind the Shield*, it says on the cover.

Up early this morning, still dark, a little slice of white moon hanging to the east. A Friday, Mother's Day weekend, how she'd be asked to stand in church with the other hordes of children belonging to the sad-eyed corsage wearing mothers, sitting down one at a time, until only the one with the most off-spring remained standing, ten, twelve, twenty-two, once. Her father's sermon with something about Heavenly Mother laced in to sweeten the guilt and sin and blood parts. Oh, Jesus, she can't bear another day.

Friday. Payday. She'd shave her legs, pull on the stocking with a run in the calf of the right leg, drive Daddy's truck down Main Street gushing with flowerpots in every storefront, park in the lot behind First Credit, go in the back way. Potty. Take her cash drawer from the dim lit vault. Check into her service area. Slip on the rubber fingertips. And stand before the black hands of a clock that clicked away the minutes of her life. A silver eye up there recording her every move, her facial expressions, eyeblinks, that her left breast is larger than her right.

Cash checks all day long and not be able to wash the money smell off all weekend, the paper cuts and eyestrain. Mom said she was feeling sorry for herself. Well maybe so. If not her, who?

Outside, the moon has risen out of her plane of view. Light in the east. Roger's letter written in his best hand, blue ink, up there between the pages of last month's National Geo, gladiators, America's Hunger Crisis, Domestic Violence During the Pandemic. A new variant that's a hundred times more transmissible than the last.

The couple below her have sex at strange hours.

Their bedposts—she guesses bedposts, what else?—knock the wall. Smell of pot. A dog barks sometimes. The caravan moves on. She's lonely. Thirty-something. Divorced. And very much feeling sorry for herself, and her estranged ex who asks for mercy.

Down on the North Rim.

They'd stayed in one of the big rooms to celebrate just after Christmas, down-season, woodsmoke in the air, and they'd driven down to Lee's Ferry where a party was rigging at the put-in. Five sixteen-foot rafts and an eighteen-, they were from Bozeman, Montana, and one of the women had inflated a white unicorn and was riding it around the eddy in a mini skirt with a glass of champagne and a red wig. They'd be on the river for New Year's and loaded six crates of Cook's champagne onto the eighteen-footer, more bubbly than she'd ever seen in her life, Joanna.

The unicorn woman passed her a joint and she'd taken a hit, gave it to Roger, who had some too, and it all got real interesting, the music and light, how it shone over the water, and the energy was with them, that anticipation before the float.

The unicorn woman bobbed around the eddy, sun in her hazel eyes, flipping the red wig, some of the Bozeman kids dancing to the music, two-stepping, arm in arm. When Roger was high, he was smiling. They hugged, wished the party well, drove to Marble Canyon Lodge and had a steak.

Just before New Year's, this big-ass storm came blowing in that same night, so they'd taken all their clothes off, turned up the heat high as it would go and got in bed, the hush on Jacob's Lake of falling snow. And when they woke it was about a hundred degrees in the honeymoon suite, three fresh feet of fallen snow outside the window. Blistering inside.

On a dare, she'd walked with him into the knee-deep powder, made a deep snow angel next to his own so the imprint's hands touched, their wispy wings. Naked as the day they were born, the cold snow burning holes through her feet, her heart.

And it kept coming, all day, the snow.

By nightfall, it had filled in their angels, and the magic had disappeared just like it always does. They argued about something small and he got sulky. In bed with her back to him, while the cold wind moaned and a layer of black ice formed on the blacktop, so that even behind the snowplow they'd spin into a one-eighty on the way out next morning, she'd thought of the Bozeman party, kids about to skid into thirty, out there camped in the snow on New Year's Eve, guzzling champagne, Unicorn Woman in her red wig and mini-skirt, flames roaring ten-feet-high on the banks of the Colorado.

The man snoring beside her.

A new year coming.

The hangover that would render them oblivious still a dream hurtling from worlds where men could know your secret name and not have to tell till the end of the world. Who could summon you from the grave, even, whether you liked it or not.

Stoner was okay now. He really was. Driving south. Back in the saddle. Touch and go back there. Rita with the hog leg. Mama's skinner. Big Rose all covered in blood, on her face like war paint, her white Nikes. A methane explosion. Nothing left at all. Nothing at all. He'd file a report, go by the books. Send a team. See what they could scratch up. The raven had put him in mind of Joanna, and the letter he'd written her in blue ink. It had done him good putting the thoughts into words. He wasn't embarrassed, Roger. No embarrassment in love. The right thing to do, writing her, saying he was sorry, meaning it. The wedding ring had been his grandmother's, who he loved. It had been instinct, his reaction. Seeing it sail into blue deep water, how she looked him straight in the face. Said, *What are you going to do about it?* Just a thing, metal and stone, all it was. Under the bridge, that water now. It had happened. No taking it back. He can live with that, Roger can. And whatever happened back there at BC¹, him and Mama, little and big Rose, Rita, Lynyrd, raven caw-cawing in the pillar of red dust, it was done now, and over. He'd be turning in his badge, enough was enough. He'd come to life as a man, do right, like he had by Little Rose today, that sound she made like a heart breaking.

He crosses the Little Colorado just outside of Cameron, the Coconino Rim shining off to the West, the Grand Canyon over there, Black Knob, Shadow Mountain. Wide open country rising toward Flag, an archipelago, island in the sky.

Hit the county seat and resign his post. Keep on going. Phoenix, Tucson, Mexico, what's to stop him. He'd have to turn in the patrol car, sure. Pick up a truck for nothing, slap a shell on it, there you go. No more dogs nor drunks nor writing tickets to derelicts for urinating in public. He's had it with all that, hasn't he? Let Joanna come find him if she has a mind to. He'd be where the wind blew, no more Mr. Bad Guy.

He overtakes the Arkies truck on the climb to Flag, in the slow lane, drifting past the exits to Sacred Mountain, Sunset Crater. Doesn't even have to run the plates, DMF 936. Arkansas. Expired tags. Dumb ass has turned the 2 for February into a 9. We'll I'll be damned. I'll just be godammned go to hell.

Hits the lights and siren, starts to radio but doesn't. You think you're so smart. Let's just have us some fun.

Dumb Mother Fucker.

37.

They take 95 back into Nevada and regain the hour they'd just lost to Mountain Standard Time, stop for gas at a crossroads named Searchlight. Little Rose is all about eating the World's Largest Steak, dousing it with A1 and Worcestershire. No one in Nevada wears a mask, it seems in the little store, paying for Fritos and a Diet Coke, the tankful of gas, Edgar out there squeegeeing the windshield, kicking the tires. Thank god for the credit card, all that stands between them and the end of the road, wherever that might be. The bathroom key has a pentagram magic markered on it, a sign Mormons use to let each other know they're Mormons. Mom has messaged her: *are you safe?*

"She was a quart low," Edgar said. "Thirty weight, right?"

A sticker from the dealership back in New Mexico, stuck just below the sun visor says 124,850. 5W20. Pennzoil. Daddy always made a big deal of checking oil with every fill up, tell the story about when MaMa died and they had to steal the rental Pathfinder down in Melbourne Beach. And when they'd stopped outside Tallahassee to fill up, the oil stick had come out dry. Empty. Zilch. In a brand new truck, no oil. The engine could have blown. So she always carried oil, just in case.

The hood slams hard when she finishes and inside the car smells like them, Edgar, Rose and Luce.

Almost dark now, the cowboy sign's all lit up, the gnarly steaks.

An enormous hunk is missing out of the state of Utah on the Road Atlas, the whole Four Corners area into Arizona, everywhere they've just been. Instead, the Eastern Shore of Virginia/ West Virginia. Crisfield, crab capital of the world. They'd met Pops there once, Mom and Dad, caught blue crab with chicken necks, so the story goes.

Edgar drives. The passenger seat has the butt heater on for some reason, the trick Dad always played on road trips, you never knew till your butt was hot.

"I've never been" Edgar says. "To Las Vegas. You?"

Rose sleeps behind them, the Martin back in the hatch now.

Luce says, "Once."

"So you know your way around?"

Far off on the horizon before them, a glow. "Poppy and Meemaw's fiftieth. We met them at Circus Circus."

"What's that?"

"I was ten or something. It smelled like cigarette smoke. Everywhere, it did."

Lake Mead National Recreation Area is out there in the dark east of Henderson, Hoover Dam, Caliente to the North, where Daddy's Fanchers had been running when they they got caught, and that was his story, the one that never ended.

"Mom's brother was there. His wife and kids."

"Never been to a casino. Not yet."

"They had a terrible fight, daddy and the wife. In the limousine."

"You rode in a limo?"

Through East Las Vegas she sees it coming, the Sunset Strip.

"For their anniversary. We had a champagne tour around the city. It was nighttime. We saw it from a distance, the city. And the woman chauffeur was a Showgirl who knew Elvis."

"What'd they fight about?"

"She said Frank Sinatra gave his grandkids hundred dollar bills on Christmas, had them stand in a line."

They drive on in—neon glittering in the eyes of hubcaps, cars parked under eaves where men stood in uniform, at attention, ready to do the deed.

"Here we are," Edgar says.

True enough. Circus-Circus. Twin white buildings with the repeated names lit up in white-bulbed letters. A neon-drenched clown, tall as a tree, offers a lollipop, black inside where the mouth should be. Arms spread wide over the entryway. A uniformed valet salutes them, his white-gloved hand stiff above his brow. Further on, a dark tunnel leads to underground parking. It's dark-thirty. They need a place to stay.

"Jeez," Rose says from the back. "Are we there, yet? The steak place?"

"Boy," Edgar says.

He's coming for them, the valet.

I don't want to go in there, her first thought, the chase already on off in Arizona, the first shots about to be fired. Duh, what's copper boy thinking? Give me a swig. He wants to play chicken. She remembered why they'd fought, Daddy and Uncle Rock's wife. She was from Texas, and Daddy'd kidded her that Texas was in the Midwest, so she wasn't southern. It was a big thing, being southern. And the wife had just exploded. She went ballistic. And they'd had to pull the limousine over with Las Vegas glowing off in the distance, Poppy and Meemaw bewildered. It was their anniversary, fifty years, they'd flown from Florida. Just what was this about? It said so in the Old Farmer's Almanac, Daddy said, Texas was Midwest.

The dark mouth curved into a smile, arms spread wide for the embrace.

Mom had told him to shut the fuck up, Daddy. And they got back in the car and drank the champagne included in the Sunset Tour, and the showgirl chauffeur told them how Don Rickles was demonic, and that she'd been the swing girl whose panties shown through in that Bing Crosby special. What was a swing girl? Who was Bing Crosby. Back at Circus Circus, they'd gone to their cigarette-smelling room, only Daddy'd quit talking. He went to play blackjack. See you later, alligator. The next day they'd driven home through a landscape dotted with volcanoes, St. George and LaVerkin and Hurricane, strange named towns on the outskirts of Zion. Paragonah. Scipio. Virgin River. Toquerville and Orderville, New Harmony. Land named by Mormons who'd been sent from Salt Lake to claim the Spanish Trail—an army of them called the Nauvoo Legion.

He took Exit 42 through New Harmony, Daddy, drove them to the Mountain Meadows Massacre Site. Middle of December, no one was there. The wind was blowing. Empty and plain. A sign said, *Where the Women and Children Were Killed* and another, *Where the Men Were Killed.* There were pointers and a big pile of rocks over where the bodies were buried. Nobody said anything. It was pretty, Mountain Meadows. Twenty miles from Nevada. Engraved on the bronze plaque: *They Were from Arkansas.*

A plastic food bag sailed past, two women in high heels that clickety-clacked on the sidewalk. The clown's neon eyes blinked, Circus, Circus. The valet stood at attention outside the passenger door. She could smell his aftershave, Luce.

"This is the place," Edgar said. "Gonna play me some poker."

"Don't forget the steak. I could eat a horse."

The car was still running, the Subaru. 8:37. Mother's Day Weekend, a special on for all mothers. Free champagne and corsage, a facial and booth time in the Pure Air Room. Free drinks and snacks in the Casino. The cheapest prime rib in town.

"We're stopping here, right?" Could have pawned the Woodmaster, had he brought it. A hundred or two, that's all he needed. That guitar?

A silver tip fired from a .30-ought six can pierce an engine

209

block, blow a hole the size of a fist out the backside. Gasoline would drip out the lifters, the sparkplugs and motorhead.

A dark spot burnt into the pavement.

"Not today," Luce said. "Let's keep going a ways."

Behind her, Rose moaned. "I was already tasting it," she says. "That steak and fries."

The spectacle fills all their mirrors as they drive away, the rear and side views, little cameo mirror on the visor. The valet standing below the clown, still as stone. Waiting to show them to the door, the dark place inside the mouth. Issue underground parking.

38.

She smells the ocean before she sees it. The same one they'd
visited when she was four and MaMa Josephine had drowned,
and she'd asked if MaMa was hungry in her casket. A long, long
time ago, there'd been wildflowers and rabbits. He'd burned
their calendar, Daddy, waded out into the surf where a whale
cow and calf swam. A bloated sea lion had washed in above
the breakers. The first time she'd smelled death. They'd laced
flowers around its neck, built a driftwood shelter, tied on a blue
tarp for the door. The wind was blowing. Inside was dark and
still, and he'd come to them there. Inside the driftwood shelter,
the smell of death had let them be, Mom and Dad and Luce.

Pink sky in the morning, sailor's warning.

They'd got the news at a rest area outside San Bernardino,
where they'd hit mountains and ski lifts reminded her of home,
all those Sundays they'd driven up the mountain, their church,
the saying went, house of the falling snow. How an as-of-yet
unnamed Arizona State Trooper had apparently been in pursuit
of a stolen pickup truck on AZ Highway 89 south of Tuba City.
He'd likely been fired upon, the Trooper. A vehicle had flipped.
There had been a fire. The offending subject was still at large.
A manhunt had been organized. The assailant was considered
armed and dangerous. The stolen truck had been located. The
subject was presumed to be on foot. More details as they arrived.

Masked Rose had gone to the bathroom. It was Edgar and

211

Luce, listening. They did not speak for a moment. They'd spent the night in the car, seats reclined, with Rose in the back hatch snoring a little, dreaming of baked potato sprinkled with Bacos and chives, caramelized onion, butter and sour cream.

"Do you think?" Edgar said.

In her heart, she knew.

"My rifle was behind the seat. Loaded."

Rose opened the back door. "I called in sick. Again. It's so irresponsible of me. What's for breakfast?"

Luce turned the radio off. She thought of the officer's car on fire, the flames of it lit up in the offender's eyes. The two boys? Louie? Yazz?

He'd surely to hell radioed for support. An eye witness had not yet come forward. More details were forthcoming. The incident was being considered homicide with a deadly weapon. The subject was armed and dangerous. Use caution. Report all suspicious sightings.

She started the car, Luce, a little sick feeling, in need, but of what? They'd put the vile clown behind them, dodged that bullet. What now? What came next? How did this play out?

She listened to Edgar try to explain. Driving off the mountain ranges past the towns and cities and dried up lakes that fell to the sea, he told her what might have happened. That what was maybe his truck, with his registration and inspection information tri-folded in the glove compartment, was maybe stolen and involved in the homicide of a State Trooper whose patrol included Coconino Country. That Yazz and Louie might have hauled off and gone too far this time. Edgar's prints were maybe on the offending weapon.

"Shit," Rose said.

"Yeah, shit," Edgar said.

And they drove in silence, stomachs growling, munching the last of the Fritos and bean dip until they hit Newport Beach, and it was impossible to go any further unless they swam.

"He gave me food," Little Rose said there at the end, facing blue water with the salt air cold on their faces. A storm had blown waves in from Tahiti, and they were breaking thirty feet high against a stone jetty.

She'd never even known waves like that could exist, Luce, loud as a freight train in Lonoke County, Arkansas while you waited at the Main Street crossing for the bars to raise and let you go.

The three of them stood there stretching their legs, backs against the Subaru warm from long driving. Daddy's guitar was under mom's beach towel, the one they'd given her when she retired from Granite School District. The initials R.H. sewn into a corner in blue thread, her gift for twenty-five years of teaching.

She cried openly, Rose.

The lifeguards wore flippers. For some reason, they did. One of them ran toward the water in big gawky strides.

And though no one might have known it or cared, Officer Roger Doyle Stoner, a Lee on his mother's side, was mourned there. At the edge of the old world or the beginning of the new, he was.

They'd found the truck, if not the boys, who'd somehow made it back on foot, reminiscent, Lynyrd thought, of the Chiricahua days of his youth, when his father'd call him by his Indian name, have him take a mouthful of creek water, run to the mountaintop and back, spit the water into his old man's hand to prove he'd nose breathed the whole way. Big Rose had filed the report, made their alibi. By some gift of Grandfather Sun Bear's blood in her veins, she'd gathered what had happened by the signs the boys had left, three slices of missing white bread, squashed-headed chicken kicked off the pile, length of green water hose, cap screwed off a whiskey bottle, Fireball by the smell of it.

Why, they'd been processing chickens, hadn't they? See the 55-gallon drum on the back patio where they'd wood-fired water for scalding. The pile of guts and feathers, cut off heads and feet. The truck had gone missing while they were processing chickens, and who on earth can keep a lookout on their front yard while doing that? Some brazen thief walk up right past your dogs, poor sick Thelma out there swollen-bellied in the drive.

Sure enough, the boys had blood on their boots, smelled to high heaven, the reporting officer noted. Louie's car flat out of gas at MaryBoy's, not a drop left in the tank, they'd had to walk home sure enough.

"See the blood on their boots," Big Rose had said. She'd shaken a chicken claw at him, the Officer up from Coconino County, investigating the theft and possible connections to the homicide of Officer Stoner, who was known to have been in the vicinity before driving back to Flag.

The gut pile had turned his stomach, the officer's.

Showed him the plucked hens, each in its own-two-gallon Ziploc in the freezer. What did he know about chickens, the plucking and drawing?

"Sent these girls to freezer camp," Big Rose said. "You care to take one?"

He said, "No thank you, ma'm."

She was good, Rose was. Always had been. The chickens had been an important part of the year, had represented hope when so much else had gone south.

Why had she processed them, the chickens? "Quit laying," Rose said. They were stubborn. Pecked each other raw."

"And where was the owner?" the officer asked.

"Of the chickens?

The truck. He'd need to talk to the owner of the truck.

He'd known her a long time, Lynyrd had. The way you can know clouds that still have it in them to surprise you, just when you think you know. The officer had her here and she knew it, Yazz and Washer standing there hang-dog, no help in their bloody boots.

"His tags were expired," Rose said. "Mr. Paris's. He was long-term parking till he got the dough to renew."

The officer looked her up and down, Lynyrd and the boys.

"And where was he now?"

"How should I know," Rose said. "I'm not Birdy's keeper."

"Birdy?"

"Looks like a bird."

The officer smiled. He couldn't help it. She had spunk, this Indian, she did. Offering him one of the dead chickens, likely spoiled from laying out half a day. All part of it, Rose's story.

"He have a phone number? A contact?"

"Uh-uh. Just shows up when he shows up."

"He pay you?"

"Works around the house. He's handy like that."

They'd found the truck, were running prints, though they were muddled. The thief had wiped the inside out with one of the sixteen packages of clean-wipes behind the seat where they'd found the deer rifle. It would all come out, sooner or later it would. His tags *were* expired. He *had* quit driving it. He wasn't from around there, Edgar Paris. Arkansas DMF 936. And even a dumb mother fucker wouldn't steal his own truck and fire off his own rifle at a cop and walk away with his registration and inspection folded in the glove compartment. Would he?

Sooner or later, they'd track him down. And when they did, Rose's story would check out, totally it would. She'd shot straight with them, it'd all check out, even the girl from Florida who'd somehow come into the story, driven all the way across the country to deliver her father's guitar to somebody who wasn't even related to her. They'd find Edgar and Rosie Paris on their little goat farm in Sooke, B.C., their own private capital of the world, little Marty, two barns and a Ford 8 N tractor, a pony and some dogs. The strait of Juan de Fuca between them and the man. They'd run from Arizona and made it. For now, they had.

The strangest thing. All of it just too far-out to make up.

He'd have to doctor the dog, poor Thelma. She'd been a good one, could understand human language just like anybody else. Go get the newspaper. Take this note over to Mama Linda. Want to go on a deer hunt? Yazzie'd admit to it, the gasoline soaked bread, look like he'd seen a ghost, come running back ragged and scared. The red-faced Washer kid. What had they got themselves into?

Big Rose knew what was what.

What to dig up and what to bury.

Now that the cop was gone, he'd have to dig a hole for all those guts and heads and claws, the black feathers that turned purple in the sunlight. The soft spot out back of the coop, use the wheelbarrow with a flat tire. Mother's Day weekend, maybe they'd go to MaryBoy's for a cold one, Rita'd bake Big Rose a cake and they could do ribs over charcoal. Frybread and potatoes. The boys would go home to their mothers and make homemade cards that said I love you and I'm sorry and no more of that for me. They'd carry it with them, maybe. See it when they shut their eyes. Go straight the way Lynyrd had when gifted with the chance.

Or not.

He felt bad for Stoner. The man had changed some there in the end, Rita waggling

Kuya this way and that, Mama with her skinner. How disarming had been his idea. Yes, it it had been methane up there, and they'd all got out free from BC^1.

A slick hunk of pink granite shining off on a rise. KIDDING was all it said, the letters cut in Times New Roman, italics.

The funniest thing.

39.

North of the jetty, a couple miles, the water lay down some, and there was beach with sun-warmed sand to ease the chill. They ate sausages from a hotdog stand with waffle fries. Rose had devoured a vanilla milkshake. She'd called Mom, Luce, and explained where she was and what they were doing, and why. Back at Melbourne Beach, where this all started, a sea-going cargo ship had lost half its load of tequila, blue agave, the good kind, and the whole island was abuzz. Shiny blue bottles of Corazon were washing in at high tide, hordes walking the breakers from Indialantic to Sebastian Inlet. Building beach fires and dancing naked. You just wouldn't believe.

"When are you coming home?"

"We just got here, Mom."

"Did you give it to him yet?"

"He won't take it."

"Why?"

"I didn't ask why."

"Ask."

"I will."

"Sell it and give him the money. You say his wife's there?"

"Rose."

"It's a pretty name."

They were asleep beside each other on the beach towel with Mom's initials, starting to burn, probably. There's sunscreen in the console, a tube of Banana Boat Dad had put there because Utah was the skin cancer capital of the world.

"You met her, Rose?"

"I did."

How could that wind be so cold with the sun full out? It occurs to Luce that they're on opposite sides of the continent, as far apart as they could possibly be and still be connected by earth.

"Yeah. Remember Living Traditions?"

They'd worked it together one May in Salt Lake, the annual festival for all ethnicities in the Wasatch Front. One whole weekend on the courthouse lawn, under tall trees, hundreds of booths with music and tapestries and dancing, the best foods on earth. They'd always take her, Mom and Dad. When she was a toddler she'd swallowed a mouthful of wine they'd snuck in a water bottle, and to this day she couldn't drink it.

"I remember."

"She was Miss University of Utah Native American. Dad introduced us. She was one of his students."

"*Her?*"

"She's here with us right now. She's having a baby."

"When?"

"Christmas."

"Like Dad," she said.

"Like Dad."

In a few days, they'd head back, take it easy, see the sights. There was Disney Land and orange groves, and that town with the Naval College where mom had lived when she was a girl and Poppy was studying to be a Captain. Death Valley and Eureka and the Redwood Forest. Hollywood. That beach where muscle men lift weights.

"You make me want to be there."

Luce said, "Don't say it."

"People that are *there* want to be *here*."

"And people who are *here* want to be *there*."

"You said it."

"We did."

Yes, she still had money on the card. Her tires were good, were they ever. She'd be careful. Say hey to Rose. "I love you."

I love you.

It was enough, always had been

"He was a Washer, I forgot to say. That boy. Back at the cave."

Loud silence rang between them, she on one ocean, Luce on another.

"Are you still there?"

"Yeah."

"He had blue eyes."

At House of Guitars, a man with a salt and pepper beard and kind eyes had said "just call me Dave" in a soft voice, "let me wash my hands," and came back drying them on a white towel. Guitars were hung on all four walls, twelve strings and Resonators, Ibanezes and Gibsons and Fenders. There were mandolins and ukuleles and banjos, signed posters by famous players, Carlos Santana, Jerry Garcia and Leo Kottke both of whom missed fingers. And one that Edgar stood riveted before even as Just Call Me Dave led Luce and Rose into the special humidified room, sanctuary to the Martins and Guilds no one could touch without permission.

He'd seen the face of the blind man on the poster before. Heard the flat-picked harmonies and arpeggios on an afternoon in Arkansas when the angels had leaned down and whispered that Edgar was a good man, that his life would be a good life, that he would find love and happiness and that thing beyond the veil men hold ever between themselves and the grave. How Coach had invited him out to his Long Pool house where the long-haired hippies had gathered in the geodesic dome. The blind man in the poster had made his guitar, the very one on his lap in the picture, sound like the world come undone, clean picking the run through the G to the C, opened up his mouth and sang, "Mama don't want no guitar picking around here," and "More pretty girls than one," and "Never would have made it through the Arkansas mud if I hadn't been a'ridin' on a Tennessee Stud." How his son, the seeing man beside him, had made Edgar's fingers on the left hand into Ellie and Amelia and Beatrice, the old blind man's names for chords, and the resulting sound in the spring of his sixteenth year had been all he'd ever hoped for in this life, coloring the spectrum of his thoughts for good and ever.

That second he heard Amelia through the door of the sanctuary. "Hey," Just Dave said, "You coming?"

It had happened. A long time ago, but it had.

Then Tina'd had to come and fuck everything up and all the rest. But all that was behind him now, Edgar. The bridge business, the cave, poor burned up Stoner, God bless his soul, he'd turned the page. He was in love and going to be a father, and maybe the angels way back when had told the truth. Maybe.

In the room, a half-dozen D-28s hung on the walls, each one hand-made in Nazareth, PA. A couple big-bodied Guilds and an antique dulcimer. There were three armless chairs—the kind for guitar players—and a stool, a barred window through which poured warm light.

Just Dave had opened the black case, taken out Harvell's instrument, the one he'd left at Tri-County Coon Club on the night Ronnie Love bit his finger off. Some story, that. Where this started.

He whistled, Just Dave. Held the body up to a milky eye and mouthed the serial number. He lay the guitar gently on his lap, produced a yellow Fender cleaning cloth and polished the face, the rosewood neck. "642551," he said, voice rising a notch on the last digit. "1998. I don't know what month. We could find out."

"January," Luce said. "The year I was born. We're the same age."

How Rose's black hair shone, despite the travel and wear and beach sun that burned him silly. She'd put on a turquoise ring, shaped like a flower. The sickness had let her be. Maybe the salt air. Something about the water.

Handed it to the Harvell girl. "It's a beaut," he said. "Can you play?"

Learn to play. The 4th instruction. *If you don't want, take to Edgar T Paris. Dinnehotso, AZ.* Here she was, she'd done it.

Luce made the E-minor, strummed five times and went to the D, her only move.

"Heart of Gold," Just Dave said. "You know the story?"

He always hammered on the minor after the D, slid into the C and back to D. Mining for a heart of gold. The song from *Harvest* that she'd no doubt heard sung from the womb, the soundtrack of her life before it was hers.

The minor was deep and sad and resonant in the small room. It reverberated through the sound holes of its sister instruments, and rose brightly to the C. There were marks from his belt buckle on the backside. He'd played for her in her high chair had wanted her to grow up in a house of music. Mom played the flute, though she gave it up.

"Story?"

"Hank's '41 D-28. Neil Young bought it at a store not unlike this one in Nashville. It's the one you hear him play in that song. Hank Williams' Martin." Just Dave tilted his head ever so lightly toward Edgar, Rose beside him. Had she started to show?

"What can I do for you?"

Just then Rose yawned, big and wide and full. Edgar reached for her ringed hand, touched the green flower. A small gesture.

They did not look like wanted people. Mother and father and unborn child. Keeping their heads down.

"How much is it worth?" Luce strummed down on the D one string at a time, the sound bright and shining. Like a happy thought, or the way you feel after some dreams. The guitar had held its tuning, she'd never turned a peg.

And then to the E-minor, a hard chord played so often that his nails had scarred the fretboard. Light then darkness.

Darkness then light.

EPILOGUE

Outside West Palm Beach there was a landfill she used to drive when the worst of the homesickness hit, and if she didn't find a place that wasn't flat to rest her eyes on she would die. It had been deep into fall by then, October, Halloween, and the weather hadn't changed. One hot, humid and then rainy day after another, she'd grown sick and tired of the beach and heavy air and kids of Haitian emigrants at Rolling Green who'd taught her to say *goodbye* and *tree* in Creole, coughing and sick and hungry, always laughing. Her favorite, Isabel, had taught her goodbye on that last day before she'd driven west.

"*Orevwa*," the tiny girl said, swiping a tear.

"*Orevwa*," Luce repeated.

"No go."

"Go."

"No orevwa."

"Orevwa."

When if she didn't find some place where the land climbed toward sky, the earth would consume her for good and ever. The landfill was bowl-shaped and anyone could just drive right in on the dirt road laced with nails so she'd had three flats since that All Hallow's when she'd found it, the hill-shaped landfill.

Because you never know, do you? what you love until you leave it. She'd grown up with mountains in every direction.

Skyscrapers that went alpenglow pink at sunset and dawn. Frost in September, and the towering snow-clad Wasatch as backdrop when the leaves turned, and three carved pumpkins burned on their front porch, that good scorched smell of winter coming. Thanksgivings and Christmases, when December snowstorms would blow your doors off, ten feet in one storm once up on Alta Mountain, so the cars were buried till springtime. January birthdays, and the light coming back in spring, forsythia blooming like crazy all down their street where guitars and dogs howled, snowfalls that covered the daffodils and made little mower tracks in the first lawn mowings.

She'd missed it. Terribly, she had.

And she'd driven west, *Orevwa.*

Like her kith and kin had forever and ever and ever. She doesn't want it to end, Luce, she doesn't. But if you go far enough, the land runs out, and then what?

Mother's Day, May 9, the day Dad lost his brother in a world she never knew that keeps on happening. Telling the beach goodbye, the ocean. Best turn back, or you might fall in. From the end of the earth, or the beginning, the land rises, Sierra Madre to Lovelock and beyond, Utah out there somewhere. Place where there are mountains, the word means. If she keeps driving, she can make it by nightfall, sleep in the desert under a field of stars. Give thanks for their mothers, Grandma Josephine and Dee, Meemaw, and her own mother back at Melbourne Beach, waiting for her, just like she'd waited for him those long nights after the fall.

She holds it to her heart, the thought of Mom alone on the stairs at the end of Third Avenue, the Atlantic spread wide before her, enough tequila to buzz the whole island washing in from deep water.

Blue bottles of *Corazon,* she'd said. It meant heart, *Corazon,* and what better way to end a day, when the faded light gave way to sea turtles, big as buffalo, harrumphing and grunting their ways up into the dunes to lay eggs in shallow holes dug by moonlight?

She reaches mom the heart message across space and time, from here to there to forever. *Please hear me, Mama, I love you, I'm coming home. No orevwa. No. I'm thinking of you, you're in my thoughts. You hear me, I know you can. Be happy for me, please be happy. I made it. I did my part. I'm coming home.*

I love you.

I love you.

I love you.

She pushes the thought, the prayer, hard as she can—with her heart, Luce pushes. It soars over what remains of BC[1] and the land of the woolly-headed Washers. Past Salt Lake and the Rockies, right down through Oklahoma into Arkansas and beyond. St. Augustine to Canaveral to the Treasure Coast stairs that fall down to the beach at the end of Third Avenue, where turtle tracks draw her mother's eye to the bright blue door of water.

ACKNOWLEDGMENTS

Thank you to the folks at Madville for all their work in seeing this project through and hopefully uniting it under one roof someday soon. Heartfelt thanks to my novel writing students for slogging along with me day in and day out, no matter what. As ever, none of this would ever happen without the support of my wife and daughter, Jill and Lyra—*thank you*. I'm grateful to the writer Rick Campbell for recognizing that the *Go Love Quartet* needed a fifth novel—or *Coda*—to close it out, so all that dynamite wouldn't be left waiting to blow under Navajo Bridge down on the Grand. My argument was that Mountain Meadows wasn't over, that it was still happening and would keep on happening until a final reckoning happened for the perpetrators. But Rick was probably right. As Edgar finally learns, how can the living hurt the dead? Not let them die. For the Poteets—my skin in the game—the explosion up in BC[1] lays them to rest, at least for me. Luce and Edgar and Little Rose and her unborn baby, they make it to California and the blue-cold Pacific in place of all those who ever set out west, and all that stands for, only to fail.

Amen.

ABOUT THE AUTHOR

Arkansas native Michael Gills is the author of thirteen books of fiction and nonfiction, including *Before All Who Have Ever Seen this Disappear* (Madville 2023), *New Harmony* (Raw Dog Screaming Press). *Burning Down My Father's House* (Texas Review Press 2023). Other works have been nominated for the PEN/Faulkner Award for Fiction and won the Southern Humanities Review's Theodore Hoefner Prize for Fiction, Southern Review's Best Debut of the Year, recognition in the Best American Short Stories and Pushcart Prize Anthology, and inclusion in *New Stories from The South: The Year's Best*. His undergraduate novel writing workshop has been featured in USA Today, and several of his students have gone on to publish books of their own, including Emi Wright's *Alegría* (Madville Publishing 2021) and Katie Sayal's *Lady of the House* (Madville 2025). Gills is a Distinguished Honors Professor at the University of Utah, where he lives in the hills with his wife of thirty-eight years, Jill.